J. T. EDSON'S
FLOATING OUTFIT

The toughest bunch of Rebels that ever lost a war, they fought for the South, and then for Texas, as the legendary Floating Outfit of "Ole Devil" Hardin's O.D. Connected Ranch.

MARK COUNTER was the best-dressed man in the West: always dressed fit-to-kill. **BELLE BOYD** was as deadly as she was beautiful, with a "Manhattan" model Colt tucked under her long skirts. **THE YSABEL KID** was Comanche fast and Texas tough. And the most famous of them all was **DUSTY FOG**, the ex-cavalryman known as the Rio Hondo Gun Wizard.

J. T. Edson has captured all the excitement and adventure of the raw frontier in this magnificent Western series. Turn the page for a list of Floating Outfit titles.

J.T. Edson

THE LONE STAR KILLERS

Originally published in Great
Britain as *Beguinage Is Dead!*

CHARTER BOOKS, NEW YORK

This book was originally published in Great Britain
under the title *Beguinage Is Dead!*

This Charter book contains the complete
text of the original edition.
It has been completely reset in a typeface
designed for easy reading and was printed
from new film.

THE LONE STAR KILLERS

A Charter Book/published by arrangement with
Transworld Publishers, Ltd.

PRINTING HISTORY
Corgi edition published 1978
Charter edition/February 1990

ISBN: 1-55773-308-2

Charter Books are published by The Berkley Publishing Group
200 Madison Avenue, New York, New York 10016.
The name "CHARTER" and the "C" logo are trademarks belonging
to Charter Communications, Inc.

PRINTED IN THE UNITED STATES OF AMERICA

10   9   8   7   6   5   4   3   2   1

For Ann and Kate, from myself and my koi carp, "Sydeny," who says they can jump into his fish-pond again any time

Author's note

As the records given to me by Alvin Dustine "Cap" Fog referring to this portion of his grandfather's career were too extensive to be covered in a single volume, while complete in itself, this book follows on from the events recorded in BEGUINAGE.

Once again, for the benefit of new readers and to save my old hands from repetition, I have given the relevant details of the floating outfit's backgrounds and special qualifications in the form of appendices.

J. T. Edson

Active Member, Western Writers of America,
Melton Mowbray, Leics., England.

CHAPTER ONE

He'll Kill You If You Do

"In the name and authority of

THE STATE OF TEXAS

To all to whom these presents shall come

GREETING:

CAPTAIN DUSTINE EDWARD MARSDEN FOG
Texas Light Cavalry, C.S.A., Rtd.

is hereby commissioned by us to act as bodyguard and protector for our distinguished foreign visitor:

CROWN PRINCE RUDOLPH OF BOSGRAVNIA

As it is known that conspirators are plotting against the life of our distinguished visitor and it is essential that his safety be assured at all costs, Captain Fog is therefore authorized to pose as an outlaw and, without prejudice to his honour and good name, to consort with known or suspected criminals in the execution of this commission.

By virtue of the authority granted through my office, I, Stanton Howard, do hereby command all law enforcement agencies within the boundaries of the Sovereign State of Texas to afford any and every assistance Captain Fog may request in the commission of this assignment.

In testimony thereof, I have hereunto signed my name and caused to be affixed the Seal of State at the city of Brownsville, Cameron County, Texas, this 16th day of June, A.D. 1875[1]

STANTON HOWARD,

Governor."

Having read through the pronouncement, mouthing some of the longer words half audibly, Town Marshal Benjamin Digbry shoved back his round-topped brown hat to scratch his head and looked in a puzzled fashion at the man who had handed the notice to him. It was a most impressively worded and official seeming document. However, in spite of its solemn content, it had been folded to just wider than the two inches' diameter of the imposing cogged-edged, embossed gold leaf Seal of State attached (when it was fully open) to the bottom right-hand corner.

Although Digbry was the head of the municipal law enforcement agency of what was fast becoming the major seaport of Texas, Corpus Christie, he was neither too intelligent nor efficient in the performance of his duties. Rather he held his appointment by virtue of his skill in a roughhouse brawl, and because his ability at handling a gun was more than the local average. Such qualities were proving no use whatsoever in the present circumstances. Taking his hand from his head, its scratching having done nothing to help him find a solution to his dilemma, he wiped his fingers on the trouser leg of his brown suit. Having done so, he tugged at the unaccustomed collar and necktie with no more beneficial results.

Middle-aged, tall, burly, heavily moustached and surly featured, the peace officer looked as ill at ease as he was

---

1. Although this is the date supplied by Alvin Dustine "Cap" Fog, the author must state that it may be incorrect. The falsification would have been carried out to avoid possible embarrassment to the descendants of certain people, whose names have also been changed, who are believed to have died more honourably than is recorded.—*J.T.E.*

feeling. Just as he was about to leave for an important social function, he had received a summons in the name of a person whom it would have been most impolitic of him to ignore. Arriving at the Edgehurst Warehouse as required, he had found that somebody entirely different was waiting for him. For all that, he had considered it advisable to refrain from raising objections to the subterfuge. He had also ensured that neither of his hands went anywhere near the short barrelled Colt Model of 1871 "Cloverleaf" House Pistol, a revolver in spite of its name, in the cross draw holster under the left side of his jacket.

Receiving no enlightenment from the only other living occupant of the large building, Digbry turned his gaze to the body which was sprawling face upwards and with arms outthrown on the floor. When he had first seen it, he had assumed that he had been called to attend to the legal side of a straightforward, if unpleasant, matter which would bring a financial remuneration for his services. However, the document he had just finished reading suggested that the affair might be much more complicated and far reaching than he cared to contemplate. In fact, it might even prove a threat to his future career as town marshal.

Clad in what appeared to be the usual brown habit, bare legs and sandals of a Mexican Catholic mission *padre*, the corpse's features—distorted by agony and a hatred that seemed out of keeping with such attire—were suggestive of some more northern European origin. Not far from the right hand lay a wicked looking fighting knife and what was clearly its sheath was strapped to the exposed left wrist. The weapon's spear point[2] was coated with something blackish that might be dried blood and could account for the fact that, despite his priestly raiment, it was necessary for two bullets to have been planted in the centre of his chest.

Failing to form any helpful deductions from the body,

---

2. "Spear point": one where the sharpened edges of the blade come together in symmetrical convex arcs. Designed for fighting, it is far less utilitarian than the "clip point" of the general purpose "bowie" type of knife, a description of which is given in Footnote 7, Appendix Three, for the benefit of new readers.—*J.T.E.*

Digbry returned his scrutiny briefly to the first communication he had ever seen from the Governor of Texas. There was no evidence of greater comprehension as he lifted his gaze to the person responsible for his perturbation. Having looked the man over from head to foot, he stared yet again at the document as if unwilling to credit the evidence of his eyes.

"*Captain Dustine Edward Marsden Fog*?" the peace officer read, making the words into a question rather than a title. "B–but that's——he's——you——he's *Dusty Fog*!"

"They call me 'Dusty' as being short for 'Dustine'," answered the man to whom the words were addressed, his accent that of a well-educated Texan. "But it's also because my hair's a sort of dusty blond colour—most of the time, anyway. Right now I've got it dyed black."

"*You* can—*You're Dusty Fog*?" Digbry croaked, changing the format of his statement to something less dangerous than accusing his informant of lying. "B–But Buck Raffles told me your name's *Rapido* Clint!"

"Well now, that could have been because *I'd* told *him* my name was *Rapido* Clint," the man replied, showing no embarrassment over having deliberately deceived another person with a false introduction. "Or do you-all reckon he'd have taken me all around this town of *yours* so friendly, telling everybody I was a hired gun looking for work, if he'd known the truth about me?"

"No, I reckon not," Digbry admitted and, with a chilling suddenness, began to appreciate the implications behind the other's identity as far as he personally was concerned. "Th–Then you *are* Dusty Fog?"

"Comes down to a right fine point, my momma prefers 'Dustine'," drawled the cause of the peace officer's apprehension, without displaying annoyance or any other observable emotion over his identity being put to question. "But 'Dusty' does for my friends. *You-all* can call me 'Captain Fog,' but we'll dispense with the 'Texas Light Cavalry, Confederate States Army, Retired.'"[3]

Although the marshal did not realize it, there was no cause

---

3. For the benefit of new readers, full details of Dusty Fog's background and qualifications are given in Appendix One.—*J.T.E.*

for his concern over one aspect of the affair. Dustine Edward Marsden "Dusty" Fog was never either surprised or particularly disturbed whenever he discovered that somebody was unable to reconcile his physical appearance with the reputation he had accrued by virtue of his capabilities in various fields of endeavour. Being a completely honest young man, he was the first to admit that he looked nothing like the image many people formed when hearing of his exploits as cavalry officer, cowhand, trail boss, or lawman.

For all his reputation, Dusty Fog was no more than five foot six inches from his tan coloured, sharp-toed, high-heeled boots to his low-crowned, broad-brimmed Texas-style black J.B. Stetson hat. He had a tanned, good-looking—if not eye-catching—face which would have impressed a more discerning person than Digbry with the strength and intelligence in its lines. There was a width to his shoulders, tapering down to a lean waist and sturdy legs, that was suggestive of exceptional muscular development. However, his clothing tended to conceal rather than display his physique. Although they were of good quality, the tightly rolled scarlet silk bandana, black leather vest, open necked dark blue shirt and the Levi's pants which hung outside the Hessian legs[4] of the boots seemed to have been handed down to him by someone better favoured. Nor, except that the marshal knew how potent he could be with them, did the brace of bone-handled Colt Civilian Model Peacemakers[5] in the cross-draw holsters of an excellently designed brown gunbelt add anything to his stature or make him more noticeable.

Listening to the small Texan's confirmation of identity, Digbry decided that the document was genuine, and then he remembered the influential people to whom the other was related. So he was disturbed by thoughts of how some of his far from legal activities had been at least suggested to "*Rapido Clint*" during their brief acquaintance.

---

4. Hessian leg: extending to just below knee level, with a V-shaped notch at the front, as on the footwear worn by Hussars and some other types of light cavalry.—*J.T.E.*

5. New readers can find an explanation of the various types of Colt Model P "Peacemaker" in Footnote 17, Appendix One.—*J.T.E.*

"S–Sure, Cap'n Fog!" the marshal said hurriedly, noticing he had not been offered the privilege of employing the name "Dusty". Running the tip of his tongue over suddenly dry lips, he forced an ingratiating grin to them. "I hope's you didn't get no wrong ideas seeing me acting so friendly with somebody the likes of Buck Raffles?"

"I *didn't*," Dusty admitted truthfully, although his meaning would have wiped away the relief Digbry was starting to feel if he had elaborated upon it. He had every honest person's aversion to corrupt peace officers. Nor was his dislike reduced by the realization that he could take no positive action against the marshal in the prevailing circumstances. "Just so long as you-all won't have any where I'm concerned."

"I won't, Cap'n Fog, I surely won't!" Digbry promised vehemently, waving the document to emphasize his concurrence. "Shucks, even without what the Governor says here, ain't *nobody*'s would take you for a —"

"*Bueno*," Dusty interrupted and continued in a coldly threatening fashion, "Because I don't need to tell a man with *your* experience just how unhealthy it could be to do otherwise."

"Huh?" Digbry grunted, looking both startled and uncomprehending.

"Take a look at it from Buck Raffles' point of view," Dusty elaborated, not in the least surprised by the marshal's failure to understand his meaning, in spite of how he had worded his previous comment. "He's Ram Turtle's *segundo* and boss gun. Which it'd give some folks one hell of a laugh should they find out that he hadn't been able to tell the difference between Dusty Fog and a *pistolero valiente*[6] called 'Rapido' Clint' just because the names are different and I've had my hair dyed black."

"Wouldn't they though," Digbry grinned, thinking of the thinly veiled contempt with which the boss gun had always treated him and pleased by the prospect.

"Only, was I you-all, I wouldn't be the one to spread the word around," Dusty warned, judging from the other's enthu-

6. *Pistolero valiente*: an exceptionally competent gun-fighter, especially one who is a hired killer.—*J.T.E.*

siasm that the context of his comment had been misunderstood. "He'll kill you if you do."

"K–Kill—?" Digbry gurgled, losing his satisfied leer.

"Getting a feller like him all riled up by setting folks to laughing at him's like stroking the head of a stick-teased diamond-back rattler, a man could get killed doing it," Dusty explained. Then, wishing to have more important matters dealt with, he went on, "Anyways, you'll likely want to know what *this* is all about."

"Huh?" Digbry said, too absorbed in considering what he had just been told to devote any thought to why he had been summoned to the warehouse.

"It's just a couple of little things, might not even strike *some* folk as being important," Dusty continued sardonically, plucking the Governor's document from the peace officer's unresisting fingers. "Such as why I had to shoot that *hombre* who's dressed like a mission *padre*—and how come there's another dead man on the floor above."

"Oh yeah, *that*," Digbry answered, still too concerned over the consequences of incurring Buck Raffles' wrath to think about his official duties. Then an understanding of what he had just heard began to sink in and, stiffening as if he had been stung by a bee, he squawked, "*Dead man*! What other dead man is that?"

"The one upstairs," Dusty replied, refolding the document. Instead of returning it to the concealed compartment at the back of his gunbelt, he tucked it into his vest's inside pocket. "His throat's been cut."

"Who is it?" the marshal asked nervously, wishing that he dared to say the words, "Did you kill him too?"

"A hired killer called 'Sharpshooter'[7] Oscar Schindler," Dusty replied. "Got a Sharps Buffalo rifle and a clear shot at where the Crown Prince would have landed if the arrangements hadn't already been changed."

"Wha-Wha–Wha—?" Digbry gobbled incoherently, trying to assimilate the latest surprising piece of news on top of all the other puzzling and alarming information he had re-

---

7. "Sharpshooter": an expert marksman carrying out the duties of a sniper.—*J.T.E.*

ceived. Ignoring what should have been the most important topic to a town marshal, all he could think to say was, "Do you mean that there prince *hombre's* not coming here?"

"Not the way he was supposed to," Dusty admitted. "I haven't touched anything. So, while you're searching this *hombre*, I'll tell you what's going on."

Moving as if in a daze, Digbry bent over the corpse and set about a task he had performed many times in the past. His puzzled expression did not show any sign of clearing as he listened to the description of the events leading up to the incident he had been called in to investigate.

Not only had Governor Howard been informed that there were two groups planning to assassinate Crown Prince Rudolph of Bosgravnia during a hunting expedition which he was going to take in Texas, the message from Congress had warned there could be serious international repercussions if this was allowed to happen on United States' soil.[8] It had been stated that the distinguished visitor must be afforded every protection and no harm must befall him.

Although the Governor could have called upon the United States' Army, the Secret Service, or his own Texas Rangers, he had asked General Jackson Baines "Ole Devil" Hardin, C.S.A., Rtd., to supply the bodyguard. Howard had already seen how competently the OD Connected ranch's floating outfit[9] could deal with a delicate and precarious situation.[10] So he had had complete confidence in their ability to cope and felt they would be even more effective than any of the official agencies at his disposal. For one thing, they were not bound by regulations and would be answerable only to their employer for any means they employed to carry out the assignment.

Shortly after his arrival in Brownsville, Dusty had been told what was wanted of himself and his companions. Almost

8. The reasons are explained fully in: BEGUINAGE.—*J.T.E.*
9. A description of a "floating outfit's" function is given in Footnote 2, Appendix Two.—*J.T.E.*
10. Told in: HELL IN THE PALO DURO, GO BACK TO HELL and THE SOUTH WILL RISE AGAIN.—*J.T.E.*

immediately Dusty had found himself the object—but not the selected victim—of an attempt to have him killed. On investigating, he had discovered that the most notorious professional assassin of Europe was in the city. Known only as "Beguinage," the killer had warned off or murdered various other people who had similar intentions towards taking the life of the Crown Prince. Before he could be located or identified, Beguinage had left for Corpus Christie to await the coming of his proposed victim.

One of the people who had been warned by Beguinage was Rameses Turtle, whose family had been prominent in Texas' criminal circles even before independence was won from Mexico in 1836.[11] Dusty had been able to obtain his co-operation. Travelling to Corpus Christie in the guise of a hired killer and calling himself "*Rapido* Clint,"[12] with the assistance of Buck Raffles, he had set himself up to draw Beguinage into the open. The condition of the corpse on the floor was testimony to how successful the ploy had been.

If Digbry had been of a discerning nature, he might have noticed an inconsistency between what he had been told earlier, and the details he had just been given regarding the participation of Turtle and Raffles. It should have been obvious that the boss gun was aware from the start of "*Rapido* Clint's" true identity instead of having been taken in by a deception.

Being so lacking in perception, the marshal was equally unaware that he was witnessing an example of Dusty Fog's personal integrity. The small Texan was keeping his word even though he knew the men to whom it had been given were ruthless criminals and unlikely to have similar scruples.

When coercing Turtle into a spirit of co-operation, Dusty had promised that nothing of a criminal nature he learned would be divulged to the authorities unless it pertained to his task of protecting the Crown Prince. It had said much for the

11. An example of this is given in: OLE DEVIL AND THE CAPLOCKS. The five volumes of the "Ole Devil Hardin" series cover Texas' struggle for independence from Mexico.—*J.T.E.*

12. When Dusty Fog's grandson, Alvin Dustine, required an alias for his undercover duties during the Prohibition era (1919–33) he too adopted the name *Rapido* Clint, as is told in: "CAP" FOG, TEXAS RANGER, MEET MR. J.G. REEDER.—*J.T.E.*

respect Turtle felt for the small Texan, who had previously got the better of him in Fort Worth,[13] that the assurance was accepted. Furthermore, as Dusty had been posing as a hired killer rather than a wanted outlaw, it was easy for Raffles to ensure he did not hear details of crimes in the making.

Realizing how Raffles—whose help had gone beyond that envisaged by Turtle—would be far more compromised than the master criminal if the truth became known, Dusty's warning of how dangerous it would be to cause him embarrassment was made to ensure Digby's reticence. The secret was safe if the marshal was frightened into silence. As far as everybody else in Corpus Christie's criminal circles was concerned, finding no gainful employment was forthcoming there, "*Rapido* Clint" had gone elsewhere in search of it.

"I had a message brought to the Portside Hotel that Schindler was here," Dusty concluded, without explaining the nature of the precautions which had been taken to save the Crown Prince from an assassination bid at long range. He was satisfied that Digby had overlooked the discrepancy where Raffles was concerned. "Figured it had come from Beguinage and must be a trap, but reckoned I could stop it being sprung. It was a close call, but I made it. It doesn't look as if he's got anything much on him, though."

While speaking, the small Texan had been watching the searching of the body. Despite his conviction that he had killed Beguinage, it was something of a relief to see how the still shape was dressed beneath the *padre's* habit. It had a collarless white shirt and a dark blue suit with the trouser legs rolled up above the knees. He had noticed Digby's annoyance when the jacket's pockets yielded nothing but a pair of socks, a collar and an already fastened necktie which would have allowed their owner to affect a change in appearance from the distinctive attire of a *padre*.

"Only this," the marshal answered, holding forward what appeared to be the kind of "vest-pocket" inkwell secretaries and clerks often carried. He clearly attached no importance to the item as he handed it to the small Texan. "Last time I saw anything like it was one I took offen a tinhorn. He used it to

13. Told in: SET TEXAS BACK ON HER FEET.—*J.T.E.*

carry some dye he had for marking the cards in the game."

"Could be that's what he used it for, this isn't ink," Dusty replied, having lifted the lid and looking at the blackish paste in the container. Then his gaze flickered to the knife by the body and he stiffened slightly. There was a hint of tension in his voice as he went on, "Whooee! Likely I've had an even closer call than I figured."

"How's that, Cap'n?" Digbry asked, not knowing the small Texan well enough to detect the change.

"Take that sheath off and give it to me!" Dusty ordered, picking up the knife. "And make sure *nobody* is careless when they handle this damned thing. That's not blood on the blade, it's some kind of poison."[14]

"P–Poison?" the marshal repeated, but the baleful glare he received put motion into his limbs and he obeyed. Accepting the sheathed weapon with some reluctance, he dropped it into the right side pocket of his jacket and said, "I'll go straight to the jail and lock it in the safe."

"*After* you've searched the body upstairs," Dusty corrected. "It's not likely he's carrying anything to tell us who he's working for, but he *might* be."

About five minutes later, after having conducted an abortive examination of Schindler's body, Dusty and Digbry left the building. While the marshal was locking the door with a key they had found on a hook inside, the small Texan looked around. There was no sign of other human life in the immediate vicinity, so they set off in the direction of the waterfront. They were almost at the other side of the street when Dusty saw somebody he recognized walking swiftly from the alley they were approaching.

Of medium height and build, with nondescript pallid and bespectacled features, the man who appeared did not have the look of belonging to the Texas range country. His round

14. The records examined by the author claim that the substance on the knife's blade was *curare*, also known as *woorali* or *urare*, but do not say how Beguinage obtained a supply. A brittle, blackish resinous extract of certain South American trees of the genus *Strychnos*, especially *S. Toxifera*, it is used by the native Indians as an exceptionally potent and swift acting arrow poison. In medical practice, it is employed as an adjunct to general anaesthesia on occasion.—*J.T.E.*

topped "Derby" hat, neat brown suit, white, stiff-collared shirt, sober necktie and low-heeled footwear were such as might be worn by a well-situated secretary, clerk or salesman in one of the major Northern cities.

Despite the man's innocuous appearance, Dusty knew he was nothing so harmless as an Eastern office worker who had been transplanted to Corpus Christie. Whether calling himself "Gustav Breakast" in Brownsville or using his current alias, "George Luncher," he was the go-between for a criminal organization based in New York and one of the factions who were plotting against the life of the Crown Prince. What was more, he had already negotiated for the services of "*Rapido* Clint."

From what happened next, Dusty discovered that he was not alone in having identified the newcomer.

"Watch him, *Cap'n Fog!*" Digbry yelled, laying great emphasis on the name he uttered.

It was also obvious that the recognition was mutual.

"Luncher's" face took on a startled expression as he heard the name by which the peace officer had addressed "*Rapido* Clint." Instantly, realizing his danger, he pressed his left elbow against his side to activate the switch of the spring-loaded holster strapped to his wrist. His right hand started across to meet the Remington Double Derringer which was emerging from the cuff of the jacket's left sleeve. What was more, he saw that the marshal—who had already received payments for services rendered—was intending to earn more by preventing the small Texan from being able to demonstrate how the name "*Rapido*," which in the Spanish of the Mexican border country meant exceptionally fast, had been acquired.

While calling a warning which had no apparent justification, Digbry also acted with a rapidity that seemed out of keeping with his normally sluggish behaviour. Shooting out his left hand, he delivered such a hard push that Dusty was sent staggering away from him.

Taken unawares, the small Texan was neither able to control his movements nor retain his equilibrium. Even as he was starting to fall, he discovered that Digbry's action which might have been intended to save his life, did in fact put him in grave danger. Having learned his true identity, "Luncher" was producing the weapon which he had detected concealed in the left sleeve on their first meeting. With his balance destroyed by the marshal's push, Dusty could do nothing to prevent himself from being shot.

CHAPTER TWO

He'll Come Looking For You-All

"I'll say one thing, Mr. Richie," Crown Prince Rudolph of Bosgravnia remarked, looking over his shoulder as the barge belonging to the captain of the United States Navy's sixteen-gun steam-sloop *Nantucket*[1] was negotiating the gap in the reef, "Whoever picked this place for us to land knew what he was about. The way the ends overlap, the entrance to the lagoon can't be seen until you're almost on it."

"Yes, sir," replied the warship's third lieutenant, who had been assigned the duty of landing the distinguished visitor in Texas. He turned from signalling for the thirty-six foot launch to follow them. "But I'll still take her in carefully, if that's all right with you. It looks like the bottom's level sand, but I'd rather not chance stoving in the barge on a rock."

"Do whatever you like," Rudolph authorized with a grin, speaking excellent English and thinking of such an accident in which he had been involved a few years earlier. "From what I remember, allowing something like that to happen to his barge isn't the best way to keep the captain in a good humour."

Not quite six feet tall, twenty-five years of age, the Crown Prince was black haired, clean shaven and handsome. The rather plain dark blue Hussar-style uniform he had donned was set off to its best advantage and his slim figure possessed surprising strength and agility. Although he exuded an aura of authority, his lifetime of receiving deference and obedience had not made him haughty or demanding. In fact, his friendly nature had endeared him to the whole of the *Nantucket*'s crew.

---

1. The class of vessel to which the U.S.S. *Nantucket* belonged also carried five thirty-pounder rifled cannon as bow and stern chasers and swivel guns, but only those prices which formed the "broadside" counted in giving a warship its "rate."—*J.T.E.*

The small country over which his family had ruled for generations was hundreds of miles from the nearest sea coast, but part of his education had been obtained whilst serving as a midshipman in the British Royal Navy. Inside four days of boarding in Europe, he had been ascending the rigging of the sloop's three masts[2] with the same facility as the sailors who normally worked aloft.

The ready acceptance of Lieutenant Richie's suggestion was typical of Rudolph's behaviour all through the voyage from Hamburg, and particularly during the events of the previous afternoon. Making for the Texas port of Corpus Christie, the *Nantucket* had been intercepted out of sight of land by another vessel of her class and Captain McKie was informed of a change in the plans for delivering the distinguished visitor. It had been discovered that there was a plot to assassinate the Crown Prince and preventive measures were to be taken. While the other steam-sloop entered the harbour pretending to be the *Nantucket*, they were to proceed southwards along the coast. Next morning, on receiving a smoke signal from an escort who would be waiting, the passengers were to be put ashore and would complete the journey to Corpus Christie overland.

There had been some protests from members of the Crown Prince's small retinue. Nor had these diminished at the sight of the proposed rendezvous. An examination of the appropriate charts had informed them that there was no town in the area to which they were directed. On arrival, it was discovered that there was no human habitation of any kind. In fact, apart from a solitary figure standing on the beach putting out the fire which had been used to signal them, there had been no sign of life at all. Nor had a search of the woodland revealed the rest of the escort, or the means by which the visitors would be taken to their destination.

In addition, another factor had disturbed Captain McKie and Rudolph's travelling companions. Having an overall length of

2. Used in this context, the word "sloop" has nothing to do with size or rigging—i.e. a single-masted, fore-and-aft rigged craft having a fixed bowsprit and carrying at least one jib, now employed principally for racing —but means a vessel carrying its broadside battery on the upper, or "spar" deck.—*J.T.E.*

three hundred and ten feet, a beam of forty-four feet and a two thousand, nine hundred tons' burden, the *Nantucket* was almost twice as long as the average eighteenth-century ninety-gun "ship of the line" while only about the same width. Offering almost complete independence over the vagaries of the wind as a means of propulsion, the funnel which rose between the fore and main masts made it an even more efficient fighting vessel and showed why the days of the wooden walled, sail-driven warships were numbered. However, despite drawing only sixteen feet three inches, there was no way it could be taken into the half mile wide lagoon beyond the wide reef which ran along much of South Texas's coastline. That aspect had been mentioned in the revised instructions, but it was claimed the ship's boats could pass through a gap and reach the shore.

Apart from there having been no gap visible, even to the lookouts at the mastheads, the fact that only one man was in sight had caused the captain and the retinue misgivings. One of the latter in particular had stated that they should disregard the change of arrangements and return to land at Corpus Christie as had originally been intended. Not unnaturally, the proposal put McKie in a dilemma. To carry it out would be in contravention of his new orders.

The solution had come from the Crown Prince. Stating that to do otherwise was out of the question as it was requested by their official hosts, he had declared his intention of going ashore. Accepting the decision, McKie had insisted on sending the party in his barge and the launch, both crews being fully armed.

Sitting at Rudolph's side, Colonel Wilhelm Liebenfrau paid no attention to the conversation with the lieutenant and kept his attention fixed on the beach. His heavily moustached, seamed features might have been carved from a block of granite for all the emotion they displayed. A big, burly man, ramrod straight despite being in his late fifties, his post in the retinue was Personal Attendant. It was of far greater importance than the name suggested, entailing the duties of bodyguard and adviser. His plain, all black Hussar's uniform and close-cropped iron-grey hair gave him a coldly authoritative look. Invariably, even in the roughest sea, he moved from place to place in a manner closer to a march than a mere walk. As he had never been seen without a sabre hanging on the slings at the left side of his highly polished belt, the wags among the *Nantucket*'s crew had spread the word that he even wore it in bed. Although he had not interfered with anybody as long as he considered the Crown Prince was being treated with the proper respect, his attitude had struck the foc's'le hands as being too much the hard-bitten martinet in the mould of their captain for their liking. It had been obvious to all hands that he had not approved of his superior taking chances when skylarking aloft, but he never commented upon the matter in public.

Side by side on the thwart ahead of Rudolph and Liebenfrau, the other two members of the retinue in the barge also subjected the shore to a careful scrutiny. Neither had been popular during the voyage, having been too filled with a sense of their respective importance as the Crown Prince's travelling companions. Taken with the emphasis each had continually laid upon his family's long history and social prominence, expecting to be accorded subservient deference on that account, this had caused them to be unpopular in the *Nantucket*'s wardroom. The lower deck had been equally disenchanted with them.

Middle-aged, of medium height and thickset, bordering on corpulence, Major the Baron von Goeringwald's face indicated he drank more than was good for him. He did not have a physique to complement his elaborately frogged and tight dark green jacket and riding breeches. It had soon become common knowledge around the steam-sloop that he made use of corsets to prevent his otherwise bulging paunch from being too much in evidence. A poor sailor, he had only been seen on the calmest of days and his normally florid features still bore a greyish tinge that did nothing to improve them. His post was *aide-de-camp*.

Slightly taller than Rudolph, with close-cropped blond hair and a tanned, handsome face marked on the cheeks with the little duelling scars which were mandatory for one of his class and background, Captain Fritz von Farlenheim was in his late twenties. He had suffered less than the *aide-de-camp* from *mal de mer*. However, being an officer of the elite Bosgravnian Blue Dragoon Guards and "First Taster" for the Crown Prince, he had displayed a complete disinterest in the *Nantucket* except as a means of transporting the entourage to the United States.

By the time the barge was three-quarters of the way across the lagoon, Lieutenant Richie decided that his precautions were needless. Standing up in the stern, he found that the water was clear enough for him to see there was nothing to endanger it beneath the surface. Further evidence of what a suitable rendezvous had been selected showed in the way that the shore fell off sharply. The barge would not touch bottom until its bow was within stepping distance of dry land. Nor would the larger and more heavily loaded launch have any greater difficulty in arriving close enough to let its occupants disembark without wetting their feet.

Satisfied that there was no cause for alarm as far as the boats under his command were concerned, Richie turned his gaze to the beach. When studying the figure by the fire with the aid of a telescope prior to leaving the *Nantucket*, the lieutenant had decided he was an exceptionally fine physical specimen. Nor, seen at closer range, was there any need for the point of view to be changed.

"Ahoy there on the shore!" Richie bellowed. "Who are you?"

"Likely my name won't mean anything to you-all," answered the waiting man, his baritone voice that of a well-educated Texan. "But it's Mark Counter. I ride for General Hardin's OD Connected ranch and Governor Howard's sent me to escort Crown Prince Rudolph of Bosgravnia to Corpus Christie."

"Asking your pardon, sir," the rearmost port side oarsman put in, also speaking with the accent of a son of the Lone Star State; albeit from a poorer level of society. "I reckon that's him. From what I've allus heard, he's close to's big and good looking as Cap'n Dusty Fog and he's been riding for Old Devil Hardin's OD Connected since the end of the war."

In every respect, the man who had introduced himself as "Mark Counter" looked as popular conception imagined Dusty Fog to be.[3] A good six foot three inches in height, he was in his early twenties and had a tanned, almost classically handsome face. Shoved to the back of his head, a low-crowned, wide-brimmed white Stetson hat with silver conchas decorating its band exposed curly golden blond hair. There was a tremendous spread to his shoulders, tapering to a slender waist

3. New readers can read the details of Mark Counter's family background and special qualifications in Appendix Two.—*J.T.E.*

set upon spread apart and immensely powerful legs. Although made from the best quality materials and tailored to fit his giant frame, his clothing was functional and that of a working cowhand. Around his mid-section, a particularly fine brown *buscadero* gunbelt carried two ivory-handled Colt Cavalry Peacemakers in its contoured fast draw holsters.

"So I've heard," Richie admitted, having served for two years in Brownsville before commencing his commission on the *Nantucket*. Raising his voice to its previous bellow, he continued, "Are you alone, Mr. Counter."

"I've got help around, making sure it won't be needed," the blond giant replied, waving his right hand in the direction of the woodland. "And as soon as you land, we can be on our way."

"That seems reasonable enough to me, Mr. Richie," the Crown Prince remarked.

After throwing a glance to his rear, the blond giant took a letter from his hip pocket. Then he advanced to where, conforming with the naval tradition of the senior ranking person being last into and first out of a boat, Rudolph was leading his party ashore.

"Howdy, sir," Mark greeted, holding out the envelope. "Governor Howard presents his compliments and sends his apologies for the change in the arrangements and for not being here in person to greet you-all. He's sent this letter of introduction which will acquaint you with the latest developments.

Setting his weapon belt—which carried a fine *épée-de-combat* in the slings on the left and a revolver in a high riding, close-topped holster at the right—into a more comfortable position before accepting the sealed envelope, the Crown Prince utilized the brief period he was taking to open it in a study of its deliverer. He was impressed by the Texan's magnificent physique and demeanour. Unless he missed his guess, there were muscles of Herculean proportions in the giant frame. The other's whole attitude suggested neither subservience, nor a deliberate attempt to display an assumption of equality. Rather it exuded the aura of a man used to mingling on close to level terms with people of influence and importance. All in all, he presented a suggestion of quiet and yet complete confidence.

"My thanks, sir," the Crown Prince had said instinctively

while taking the envelope. Breaking the seal, he extracted and read the contents. Having done so, he passed the sheet of paper to Liebenfrau and went on, "I see that I'm to put myself in your hands, Mr. Counter."

"We've been told to keep you-all alive, sir," Mark answered, having drawn conclusions of a complimentary nature from his equally careful scrutiny of the royal visitor and hoping they would prove to be correct. "So the Governor figured letting us handle things our way would give us the best chance of doing it."

"*Us?*" the Crown Prince queried, looking pointedly around the beach and at the apparently deserted woodland beyond it.

"Like I said just now, I've a couple of *amigos* on hand," the blond giant drawled. "You'll meet them on the Coast Road back of the trees."

"Very well. I'm in your hands," Rudolph said cheerfully. "And now allow me to present you to my party. This is my Personal Attendant, Colonel Liebenfrau."

"Colonel," Mark responded formally, studying the iron hard face and deciding that there stood a man to be reckoned with, as he and the Personal Attendant shook hands.

"My *aide-de-camp*, Major the Baron von Goeringwald," Rudolph went on.

"Baron," Mark greeted.

"Mr. Counter," the Baron acknowledged, stiffening to a brace and clicking his heels in the Teutonic fashion without offering his hand.

"And Captain von Farlenheim," Rudolph concluded, omitting the slender blond's title of "First Taster" as he did not wish to waste time explaining its meaning. "Whose uncle I believe you know."

The blond giant had acted in the accepted formal manner while responding to the first two introductions, even to the extent of employing von Goeringwald's title, "Baron" as it took precedence over his military rank under the circumstances. However, despite his obvious knowledge of etiquette, there was a brief and yet noticeable pause before he addressed the third member of the Crown Prince's retinue. He had already recognized a certain family resemblance when watching the barge approaching, but it was not until they were face to

face that he realized how very close was the likeness to another man with the same surname he had met recently at the
residence of the uncle to whom the Crown Prince had referred.

"My apologies for staring, Captain," Mark said, after a
moment. "But I couldn't help noticing how closely you fea-
ture Alex von Farlenheim. We met at your uncle's place in
Brownsville. Are you-all brothers?"

"*Cousins!*" the "First Taster" snapped, his normally excellent English given a harsh Germanic timbre as he made the
correction, and his bearing implied that he wished he could
disclaim all relationship. "Not *brothers*."

"Come now, Fritz," Rudolph put in, employing their native
language. "You can't help the facial resemblance and everybody knows it was Alex who was responsible."

"Whatever Your Highness says!" von Farlenheim answered, also in Bosgravnian and with no obvious sign of un-
bending. Reverting to English, he addressed the blond giant.
"I trust my aunt and uncle were in good health when you last
saw them?"

"Why sure," Mark confirmed, having no idea of what had
passed between the royal visitor and the captain. "They send
their respects and hope you'll be able to visit with them before
you go back home."

"What is your official capacity, Mr. Counter?" Liebenfrau
cut in, before von Farlenheim could reply, his accent more
heavily Teutonic than that of the other three. "Are you in the
United States' Army?"

"No, Colonel," Mark answered. "I served as a lieutenant
under General Bushrod Sheldon during the war, but that was
in the Confederate States' Army."

"Are you a law enforcement officer of some kind?" Liebenfrau suggested.

"Just a cowhand," Mark drawled, without explaining that
he had worn a peace officer's badge on occasion.

"I'm not sure that I understand," Liebenfrau declared.
"Why have *you* been sent to act as our escort?"

"Seems like Governor Howard figured General Hardin's
men could guard His Highness better than either the Yankee
Army or peace officers," the blond giant replied. "He asked

for us, anyways. And I've been sent along to make a start at doing it."

"What arrangements have been made?" the colonel barked. "What force do you have at your disposal?"

"There are three of us—" Mark began, glancing at the approaching launch.

"Only *three*—?" von Goeringwald snorted indignantly, bringing the Texan's attention to him, but the words died away as Liebenfrau directed a prohibitive glance at him.

"That'll be enough, way we're handling it," Mark stated.

"And what way is that?" the Personal Attendant inquired.

"There's a wagon waiting on the Coast Road, back of the trees there, to take whatever baggage you've got along with you," Mark explained, wondering what had been out of the ordinary about the second boat. He had noticed something in his interrupted glance, but could not decide what it had been. "We've got some clothes that are a whole heap less conspicuous than your uniforms and you-all can change into them while we're loading up."

"Change?" Liebenfrau repeated. "Into what?"

"Cowhand clothes something like mine," Mark answered.

"*Cowhand* clothes?" von Goeringwald snapped. "Do you mean that you expect His Highness to make his first public appearance in your country wearing the dress of a commoner?"

"Well now, seeing's we don't have them over here, I can't say's I've ever seen a 'commoner,'" the blond giant drawled, although he knew what the term implied. "So I wouldn't know how one would dress. I've got cowhand clothes in various sizes to help get you-all into the Blaby mansion without attracting too much attention."

"It isn't right, or fitting, that His Highness should enter the first town he visits in the United States in such a manner!" von Goeringwald protested. "He must make his entrance with all the ceremony befitting one of his rank."

"Even if doing so could set him up to be killed?" Mark challenged.

"There is no danger of *that*," the Baron declared, slapping his gauntlet-encased hand against the revolver which he carried on the right side of his weapon belt. "We of His Highness's entourage can protect him, even if *you* are unable to do so."

"Against a man with a rifle that can kill at close to a mile and who can shoot well enough to do it?" Mark said dryly, not bothering to comment upon the unsuitability of the Bosgravnians' high riding holsters—each with its flap secured by a metal pin attached to the body of the rig—if a rapid extraction of the revolvers should become necessary. "Because there's a *hombre* in Corpus Christie who has one, is good enough and has been paid to kill His Highness."

"You *know* he's there?" growled Liebenfrau, silencing the *aide-de-camp* with a glare. "Then why hasn't something been done to apprehend him?"

"All we know for sure is that he's around and that he's been hired to do the killing," Mark replied, in a more polite tone than he had employed when speaking to the Baron. "We don't know exactly where he is, but that's being worked on. Which's why we're playing things this way."[4]

"Then, for all you know, he may not be in the town," Liebenfrau pointed out. "He could even have followed you *here*."

"He didn't, we made sure of that," Mark declared with complete confidence. "Only the Governor and us boys from the OD Connected know what's doing. He'll be hid away somewhere in town, waiting to cut loose when His Highness comes off the boat."

"Then why do we have to change clothing?" van Goeringwald demanded.

"We won't make it to Corpus Christie *before* he finds out he's been tricked," Mark explained, his voice hardening. "Which, unless he's been found and hawg-tied first, means he'll come looking for you-all, Your Highness. Not one of you'll pass, even at a distance, as being from Texas in those uniforms."

"We're in *your* hands, Mr. Counter," Rudolph put in firmly and a smile flickered on his handsome face. "So we will do as

4. Even before learning of Oscar Schindler's presence in Corpus Christie, Dusty Fog had envisaged the possibility that a "sharpshooter" might be employed to carry out an assassination attempt at long range. So he had suggested precautions should be taken. Such was the importance attached by Congress to ensuring the Crown Prince's safety that the measures recorded in this chapter were authorized without hesitation.—*J.T.E.*

you wish. In fact, I for one will be most interested to see how Colonel Liebenfrau will look dressed as a—*cowhand*—wasn't it you said?"

"That's what folks down here in Texas mostly call us, unless it's something worse," Mark replied, appreciating how the Crown Prince's words had made his task easier. "Which it most time is and's usually deserv—"

"I hope that the lady's presence won't make too much difference to your arrangements," Rudolph said, noticing that the blond giant was looking at the launch and guessing why he had stopped speaking. "She and her maid are accompanying us."

"Not too much," Mark admitted, realizing that he had caught a glimpse of the two women during his earlier interrupted glance at the boat. "They'll have to ride in a chuck wagon, not a coach."

"That won't worry Freddie," the Crown Prince declared.

"*Freddie*?" Mark repeated.

"Lady Winifred Besgrove-Woodstole," Rudolph elaborated and noticed the blond giant stiffen momentarily. "Is something wrong?"

"No," Mark answered. "It's just that I wasn't expecting a lady to be with you."

While that was true, it had not caused the Texan's reaction. He was wondering what Dusty Fog would make of the latest development.

Even as the thought was entering Mark's head, his ranch's segundo and good friend was for the second time in less than an hour facing a situation fraught with peril.

CHAPTER THREE

I Thought He Meant To Kill You

Having delivered the push that was putting Dusty Fog's life in jeopardy, Benjamin Digbry demonstrated one of the reasons why he had been appointed town marshal of Corpus Christie. For all his lack of more desirable qualities, he was a reasonably competent gun handler. Flashing swiftly across, his right hand disappeared briefly beneath the left flap of his jacket and emerged holding the Colt Model of 1871 House Pistol. Its three inches-long barrel and the four-shot cylinder in the form of a cloverleaf made it a compact and easily concealed weapon, factors which had done much to enhance his local reputation as being very fast on the draw.

Closing his right thumb and forefingers around the Remington Double Derringer's "bird-head" butt, the man who was currently calling himself "George Luncher" began to pluck the twin superposed barrels from the U-shaped grip of the spring-operated wrist holster's carrying rod. While doing so, he was relieved to notice that the peace officer was also drawing a weapon. He was aware of the limitations as well as the advantages of the way in which he was armed. Less than five inches in overall length, and flat, the Double Derringer was an even better concealment device than the Colt House Pistol. However, the qualities which created this also gave it a very limited potential for accuracy at any but the shortest range.

Considering that he was beyond the distance at which the Remington was effective, "Luncher" felt that Digbry's help was most desirable. The small Texan might not be the hired killer "*Rapido* Clint," but that did nothing to render him harmless. From previous visits and during his present sojourn in the Lone Star State, "Luncher" had heard too much about the capabilities of Captain Dusty Fog—and his antagonist could be none other—to underestimate the extent of his peril. Before he could be sure of making a hit, he would need to move closer. Such a respite might give the other sufficient time to recover from the marshal's push and defend himself.

Drawing back the Remington's hammer to fully cocked, "Luncher" began to advance. He was so confident of having Digbry's support that the full implications of what he was seeing did not strike him at first. Being aware of just how much authority his organization wielded in and around New York, he could not believe that a man he regarded as a dull witted country yokel would dare to double cross him. So it was with a sense of disbelief that he became aware of something alarming.

The peace officer's weapon was *not* being turned in the direction of the small Texan.

Ever an opportunist, Digbry offset a lack of intelligence with an abundance of low cunning. He had appreciated the ramifications of the situation as soon as he had seen how "Luncher" reacted to finding him with Dusty Fog. When he was asked for details regarding "*Rapido* Clint's" past activities and reputation, he had been informed of the Easterner's desire to obtain the "hired killer's" service. Rather than admit to a complete lack of prior knowledge, he had made up enough "facts" to convince "Luncher" not only that "Clint" would be worth hiring but that they were old acquaintances. So he had anticipated that his own dishonest activities might be exposed to the man he now knew was Dusty Fog.

With that factor foremost in his thoughts, the marshal had reached a hurried decision upon what type of action was in his best interests. Knowing the kind of people who were the small Texan's kinsmen and friends precluded any thought of loyalty to "Luncher." The last thing he wanted was for one member of the OD Connected's floating outfit in particular investigating an incident in which Dusty Fog had been killed or even injured.

There was only one other alternative!

Shock twisted at the Easterner's face as he watched Digbry's Colt swinging into alignment on him. Flame and white smoke from the ignited black powder gushed awesomely from the muzzle. Reeling back a couple of steps as the .41 caliber bullet struck him in the left shoulder, he neither fell nor dropped his own weapon. Even as he was about to do the latter, hoping that the possibility of his surrender would make Digbry turn on the small Texan, he was too late to save his life.

Acting as any trained gun-fighter would under the circumstances, the marshal cocked the Colt and took a more careful aim. Turning loose another bullet, he sent it into "Luncher's" head. Watching the Double Derringer flying from a lifeless hand as its owner pitched over backwards, he knew that his secret was safe.

"Are you all right, Cap'n Fog?" Digbry asked, trying to sound solicitous, as he turned and went to where the small Texan was sprawling on the ground.

"What the hell happened?" Dusty demanded, rolling into a sitting position and looking from "Luncher's" body to the approaching peace officer.

"I recognized him from what one of my informers told me," Digbry answered, deciding there was more recrimination than gratitude in the small Texan's tone. He had already thought up what he considered to be an acceptable excuse for his actions. "He's a hired killer from New York. Here, let me help you up. I'm right sorry I had to push you so hard, but I knew you weren't likely to know who and what he was. I got told he'd been brought in after somebody and thought it might be you."

"Looks like you-all've saved my life in that case," Dusty drawled, coming to his feet without offering to accept the assistance of the marshal's outstretched hand. "I'll not forget this. *Gracias*."

There was a self-satisfied smirk on Digbry's face as he returned the Colt to its holster and watched the man he had "saved" walking towards the body of his victim. He was delighted by the way in which the situation had turned out. Not only had he averted any betrayal by the Easterner of their illicit connections, the manner in which this was accomplished appeared to have earned him Dusty Fog's approbation.

The marshal would not have felt so smug if he had realized that the small Texan was far from being fooled and anything except grateful. Having guessed at the motive behind the killing, Dusty also doubted whether he would be able to prove it had been a deliberate and premeditated murder. For all that, he was determined to find some way in which he could at least cause his "rescuer" to be removed from public office.

Turning aside his thoughts of dealing with the corrupt peace officer until a more opportune moment, Dusty knelt by "Luncher's" body. He wanted to try and verify his supposition with regards to what had brought the Easterner to the vicinity of the Edgehurst Warehouse. Before leaving the Portside Hotel in response to the message which he had suspected was leading him into Beguinage's trap, he had taken the precaution of informing the desk-clerk of his destination.[1] Although he had primarily meant for the information to be available in case any of Governor Howard's staff came looking for him, it had been given to "Luncher."

Which raised an interesting point!

Why had the go-between for the criminal organization and one faction of the Crown Prince's enemies visited the hotel?

Having considered the point and reached a conclusion, Dusty started to search the body. His examination produced no clue as to the identity of "Luncher's" employees, nor where he was staying in Corpus Christie, but it confirmed the small Texan's theory of his reason for coming to the warehouse.

"Whooee, Cap'n Fog!" Digbry ejaculated, staring avariciously at the contents of the wallet taken by the small Texan from the inside pocket of the corpse's jacket. "He's toting a fair sized wad of money."

"There's four hundred dollars here, marshal," Dusty answered, having counted and replaced the bills he had extracted. "It's the rest of the advance payment I asked for as '*Rapido* Clint.'"

"Looks like he was going to—" the peace officer began, stopping as he realized that the comment he was in the process of making would expose too much of his association with "Luncher." "How'd you reckon he got hold of it, Cap'n?"

"Maybe he killed the *hombre* I've been dealing with," Dusty suggested dryly.

"Yeah," Digbry agreed, so pleased with the thought that he had avoided arousing suspicion he failed to notice the irony in the

---

1. The author had not learned of this precaution when he was producing the manuscript for BEGUINAGE. It only came to light while we were examining the rest of the documents received from Alive Dustine "Cap" Fog.—*J.T.E.*

tall Texan's tone, "Sure, Cap'n. That must be what's happened."

Paying no attention to the marshal's comment, Dusty considered the implications suggested by finding the money. Clearly "Luncher's" principals had accepted "*Rapido* Clint's" terms, but there might have been an even more urgent reason for him to be sought out than merely to confirm the deal. Perhaps the faction who had hired the Easterner had learned, or guessed, that the arrangements for the arrival of the Crown Prince had been changed. In which case, they could be wanting the assassination to take place earlier than was originally intended.

Because of Crown Prince Rudolph's popularity among his subjects, to whom he had promised sweeping reforms in Bosgravnia's laws, the two factions who were plotting against him had each originally required that his death was to be made to appear accidental. However, as Oscar Schindler's presence in the warehouse had suggested, the radical and anarchist contingent—having no desire to see their cause weakened by a beneficent régime—were now willing to let it be known he was murdered and hoped to lay the blame on the aristocrats. So it was possible that the latter coterie, who had no desire to see their power and authority diminished by the proposed reforms, might be contemplating a double bluff by asking for an obvious assassination which could be blamed upon their opponents.

Unfortunately, "Luncher's" killing had prevented Dusty from satisfying his curiosity. Nor, if his suspicions regarding their identity was correct, would the Easterner's principals be fooled into thinking he was "*Rapido* Clint." Digbry's actions had closed the gate upon the means by which he had hoped to expose members belonging to one faction of the royal visitor's enemies.

Nothing of the small Texan's feelings showed as he returned the money to the wallet and stood up. He was hard pressed to hide his revulsion where the corrupt peace officer was concerned, but forced himself to do so. There was still work for him to do and Digbry could help him. Although the anarchists had failed with Schindler and the aristocrats no longer could call upon the services of their go-between with the New York criminal organization, neither faction would allow the setbacks to make them give up. So the threats to the Crown Prince's life were still far from over. However, he considered that his task would be far less difficult with Europe's "premier assassin" lying dead in the warehouse.

Thinking of Beguinage in conjunction with his earlier speculations, Dusty recollected a subject which had intrigued him in Brownsville. The assassin had killed one adherent of each faction and warned off others, which suggested he was not in the employ of either group. It seemed that there might be yet a third party with designs upon the life of the royal visitor.

"You-all'd best hold on to this *four hundred* dollars," the small Texan stated, holding out the wallet and laying great emphasis upon the sum of money it contained. Indicating the body, he went on, "Do you know where this jasper's staying in town?"

"No," Digbry replied truthfully, although he was more concerned with trying to think of a way in which he might be able to convert at least a proportion of the wallet's contents to lining his own pockets. "That informer of mine just said's he'd seen him around the waterfront."

"Maybe your informer's found out where he's bedded down by now?" Dusty suggested, so helpfully that he might have believed such a person existed. "How about us going and asking if he has?"

"Yeah, we could do th—" the marshal commenced. Then he produced a reasonably well simulated look and gesture of annoyance, going on, "Blast it, we can't though. He left on that boat's sailed this morning."

"Now isn't *that* too bad," Dusty consoled, making his pretence at resignation sound equally genuine. Nodding at the alley from which "Luncher" had come, he continued, "The shooting'll bring folks and it's best you and I aren't seen together just now. I'll drift along and sort of nose around for a spell to see if I can find anything about this yahoo. Say what you like about this, but don't mention who I really am."

"Sure thing, Cap'n Fog," Digbry assented, doubting whether the other would be any more successful than he had been in learning where the Easterner had been staying. "I'll tend to things here. When'll I be seeing you again?"

"At the Blaby mansion for the reception, unless something turns up before then," Dusty suggested, although the words came in the form of an order. "You-all can give the Governor that four hundred dollars and we'll tell him all we've learned."

"Freddie, I would like to present you to the gentleman who is responsible for our safe delivery to Corpus Christie, Mr. Mark Counter," Crown Prince Rudolph of Bosgravnia introduced. "Mr. Counter, the Right Honourable Lady Winifred Amelia Besgrove-Woodstole."

"My pleasure, ma'am," the blond giant said, taking the hand that was extended and hoping his skill as a poker player would be sufficient to prevent his feelings from showing.

Having a keen eye for members of the opposite sex, Mark had decided that the first of the two young women to land from the U.S.S. *Nantucket*'s thirty-six-foot launch was an exceptionally fine specimen. However, hearing her full name was adding to the puzzlement which he had experienced when the royal visitor had first spoken of her.

Five feet seven in height, the young woman to whom Mark had been introduced was a honey blonde in her late twenties. She had a regal beauty which enhanced the patrician distinction of her features. Sensibly dressed in a brown tailored two-piece costume, her hair was drawn up into a large bun and held in place by a net at the back of her neck. The jacket was severely, almost masculinely, cut with no lace trimming. In spite of having an attached collar, the neck of her white shirt-blouse was decorously open. Showing from beneath the hem of the long, flared skirt were brown shoes which would be suitable for walking or riding on horseback. The attire neither concealed nor sought to show off a magnificent figure. Her whole bearing was suggestive of birth and breeding, implying self confidence that was far from over bearing or snobbish.

Whatever Mark's misgivings might be with regard to the young woman, they were not shared by the crew of the *Nantucket*. When the scuttlebutt[2] had passed around that a for-

2. "Scuttlebutt": a rumour. From the "scuttled," lidded, cask containing drinking water for the crew. This served as a gathering point at which the hands from the various divisions and "parts of ship" could meet and exchange gossip.—*J.T.E.*

real, genuine English Lady—there had soon come to be a heavy emphasis on the capital "L"—and her maid were to be part of the Crown Prince's entourage, there had been diverging views on the subject.

Ever conservative, the older foc's'le hands had been convinced that no good would come of the arrangement. It had been predicted gloomily by them that, even if bad luck failed to develop, there would be so many restrictions—such as smoking, chewing tobacco, spitting and the use of profanity all being prohibited—that life on board would not be worth living. Captain McKie had warned all hands to watch their language, state of dress and general behaviour, but she had demonstrated a satisfying tolerance when a slip was made in her presence. Without letting it be considered that she was interfering with the ship's discipline, the Lady had managed each time to intercede on the offender's behalf and save him from punishment.

Like the Crown Prince, the Lady had soon become a universal favourite. She had the rare quality of being able to associate with men, yet avoid raising hopes which could never reach fulfilment. Even the most barnacle-encrusted seadogs, officers and enlisted men alike, were willing to concede she made a better shipmate than they had anticipated. For all that, her exact status in the entourage remained a mystery. If it was for the purpose which came most readily to mind, there had been no evidence during the voyage. The marine sentries who were in a position to know claimed no clandestine meetings had taken place after nightfall. Nor were the foreign servants any more informative. They had insisted that the Lady was merely an acquaintance of their master, well connected in British society, to whom he had offered passage when learning she wished to visit the United States. Such was her popularity that it went hard on the few who had dared cast doubts upon her virtue.

In spite of various hopes expressed by some of the younger, more imaginative and lecherous of the foc's'le hands, the Lady's maid had proved as unattainable as her mistress. About the same age as the Lady, Florence Drakefield was some three inches shorter and had a buxom figure from which no formal black and white uniform could detract. Shortish red-blonde hair formed a curly halo to a pretty face bubbling with merriment. Yet, while friendly enough, she had never mingled with any section of the crew unless the circumstances were completely decorous. According to the entourage's male servants, she was well able to ensure her wishes were respected regarding the avoidance of physical contact.

"Charmed, Mr. Counter," the Lady responded, studying the blond giant as they were shaking hands. "But you seem surprised and puzzled."

"Like I told His Highness, ma'am," Mark replied, "I wasn't expecting a lady along."

"I hope my being here won't make things too difficult?" the Lady said, still watching the Texan quizzically. "But when I heard the rest of the party were being landed, I couldn't resist the chance of setting foot on dry land again. Of course, if my presence is inconvenient, I can always go back on board—"

"There's no need for that, as long as you don't mind riding in a chuck wagon instead of a carriage," Mark drawled, glancing to where the launch's crew and four men in military uniforms were unloading a small amount of baggage. I'll tell you why we asked for you to bring that from the ship while we're walking to the wagon, sir."

"I had wondered about it," the Crown Prince admitted. "Shall we go?"

"Any time you're ready," Mark agreed.

"Mr. Counter," Liebenfrau put in. "I will be sending Captain von Farlenheim and three men as an advance guard."

"Do whatever you reckon's best, Colonel," Mark replied, showing no resentment. "Go through that gap and there's a clear trail to the Coast Road."

"Send your three best men with Captain von Farlenheim, Mr. Richie," Liebenfrau ordered. "Tell them to keep their eyes open. Have the rest help our servants with the baggage."

"You must excuse the Colonel," Rudolph remarked, as he accompanied Mark and the Lady along the path a few yards behind the advance party. "His manner is abrupt, but he acts always with my best interests at heart."

"Why sure," the blond giant replied, watching as von Farlenheim led the three sailors over a fair-sized tree trunk which had fallen across the trail. "He strikes me as being a right good man to have at our back."

"He's all of that," Rudolph declared, glancing over his

shoulder to where Liebenfrau was following with Baron von Goeringwald. Then he indicated the dense woodland on either side of the trail. "Is this the kind of country we'll be hunting in?"

"Nope," Mark answered. "We'll be taking you to more open woods further inland, the sport'll be better there."

"Did you select the landing place, Mr. Counter?" the Lady inquired.

"No, ma'am," the blond giant admitted. "Why?"

"Nobody in the steam-sloop knew about it," the young woman explained, gazing into the big Texan's handsome face as if trying to read the thoughts behind it. "But I have the feeling that this isn't the first time people—or goods—have been landed here."

"It isn't," Mark conceded. "Way I heard it, cargoes used to be dropped off here after they'd been run through the Yankee blockade during the war."

"Only during the war?" the Lady challenged, with a smile.

"There'd be no call to run a blockade when one wasn't being imposed," Mark pointed out, also with a smile.

"It would be a jolly useful place for smugglers to land contraband, though," the Lady commented. "If you have such things in America, that is."

"I've heard tell of them," Mark drawled, but had no intention of betraying a confidence by telling who had selected the landing place.

"The reef looks to be unbroken from out at sea," the Lady continued, hoping to satisfy more than a casual interest by keeping the blond giant talking. She sensed that he had misgivings where she was concerned and waited to learn what was causing them. "Unless one knew the secret—"

While the discussion had been taking place, Rudolph had drawn slightly ahead of the Lady and the blond giant. Reaching the fallen tree, he noticed that the advance guard were turning a bend and had gained almost thirty yards lead on them. Then, as he stepped on to the fallen tree's trunk, a figure erupted from among the bushes and alighted, drawing two long-barrelled Colt 1860 Army revolvers in a lightning fast motion, not twenty feet in front of him.

CHAPTER FOUR

We Don't Need "Clint" to Kill Rudolph

"Six hundred dollars!" Alex von Farlenheim barked in explosive German, glaring across the table at his companion and speaking loudly enough to make the other dozen occupants of the Portside Hotel's dining-room look in their direction. "You gave 'Breakast' *six hundred dollars* as an advance payment?"

Despite realizing that the successful outcome of the assassination plot depended upon working in close conjunction with the young Bosgravnian, but yet ever intolerant when her actions were questioned by somebody she regarded as being of inferior status, a frown briefly creased the beautiful features of Charlene, *Comtesse de* Petain. Coming and going swiftly, but not unnoticed, it served as a warning—although he needed none—of the hardness that lay beneath the expression of the somehow seductive innocence which returned and supplied a clue to her true, ruthless nature.

Slightly over five-foot-seven in height, Charlene's creamy-skinned face and the firm-fleshed "hour-glass" contours of her statuesque figure made her seem considerably younger than her actual age of thirty-five. Nor could the "walking-out day dress" she had on conceal the eye-catching, voluptuous curves. Not that it was intended to do so. Despite being more decorous in lines, the tight cream jacket-bodice—its long *basque* forming an overskirt—displayed the mound of her bosom and slender mid-section as effectively as a ball gown with an extreme décolleté. The primrose-yellow waistcoat-front's V-neckline had no chemisette to form a high ruffle collar. Fitting snugly at the elbows, the three-quarter-length sleeves opened out to end in large frilled cuffs and long suède gloves emerged from them. Caught up at the sides, the long-trained overskirt had its front falls taken into pleated draperies. Worn low over the forehead in a frizzy fringe, her brunette hair was brushed back into a chignon which left her ears uncovered. The straw hat perched on it had a wide brim and small crown with ribbon trimmings which passed beneath the chignon and formed a shawl-shape around her neck. Lying on the table were her folded primrose and blue parasol and a large matching fan.

Apart from his attire being civilian and the scars on his cheeks forming a slightly different pattern, von Farlenheim's physical appearance was almost identical to that of his cousin Fritz—two years his senior—who was accompanying Crown Prince Rudolph. A white straw "planter's" hat, bought in Brownsville as being better suited to the local climate, was on the table in front of him. He had on a tight-fitting, waist long brown jacket, frilly bosomed white silk shirt and a dark blue cravat of the same material. Figure-hugging, his tan-coloured riding breeches disappeared into well-polished black Hessian boots. His weapon belt was of the Bosgravnian Army's pattern, carrying a Colt Cavalry Peacemaker in its holster, but without a sabre attached to its slings. All in all, his garments emphasized a masculine virility as effectively as the *Comtesse's* costume proclaimed her feminine pulchritude. Like her, he made use of his physical attributes as a means of attaining his ends with members of the opposite sex.

"It would be advisable to keep your voice down, Alex," Charlene suggested, forcing herself to speak in something milder than the tone she wished to employ. Her German was fluent, but with a noticeable French accent. "Somebody might be able to understand you. I would have consulted you if there had been time, although the Council have given *me* their authority to act as I see best for our Cause. But when 'Breakast' told me that the man 'Clint' would accept no other terms, I had to agree to make sure that we secured his services."

"Why do we need him?" von Farlenheim demanded, but in a much lower voice.

Sitting ramrod straight in his chair, the young Bosgravnian showed little sign of having been mollified by the *Comtesse's* explanation. To one of his upbringing and mentality, the suggestion that a member of the "weaker sex" should be other than subservient and in a subordinate capacity was practically heresy. So he had never been enamoured of the knowledge that, as she had just reminded him, to all intents and purposes their fellow conspirators had appointed her—a *Frenchwoman* —as his superior in the attempt to assassinate their country's hereditary ruler. He was aware that she had not hesitated to make major decisions without consulting him in the past. Furthermore, he suspected that on this occasion she had deliberately delayed contacting him until after she had made her arrangements with the man they knew as "Gustav Breakast."

Up until the matter which had elicited von Farlenheim's indignant comment, despite neither of them having any liking for the other, his first meeting with Charlene since his arrival in Corpus Christie had been progressing amicably. Nor had the condition been brought about entirely by a mutual remembrance that they would have to work in better harmony than had been the case of late.

Various events in Brownsville had produced unsatisfactory results. While the blame for some of the mishaps could be laid upon the *Comtesse*, von Farlenheim was aware that on one occasion at least he too had failed to show in a good light. When he had been rendered *hors de combat* by a trio of drunken cowhands, it had fallen upon Mark Counter to save Charlene from being molested by them. Claiming that doing so would offer an opportunity to gather information, she had used the incident to make the blond giant's closer acquaintance and had travelled to Corpus Christie in his company. Declining an invitation to go with him to collect the horses for use on the hunting expedition, she had taken advantage of his absence to meet and bring von Farlenheim up to date on what had happened since their separation in Brownsville.

The young Bosgravnian's improved humour prior to being told of the advance payment had stemmed from it having become obvious that the *Comtesse* had failed to learn anything worthwhile from the big Texan, or his companions. While he appreciated that her association with members of the Crown Prince's escort could prove beneficial to their purposes, he had found a certain satisfaction in discovering that it had not yet produced any positive results.

"For two excellent reasons," Charlene answered, still contriving to sound much less irritated than she was feeling, but she could not prevent the fingers of her right hand from drumming on the table near the fan. "Firstly, 'Breakast' assures me that there is no better man than 'Clint' available in Corpus Christie. Secondly, which is even more important, some of those anarchist scum are here and have already offered to hire him. Not only must we prevent that from happening, we can use him to find out if they have anybody working among us and to get rid of them for us."

"How do you know *they* have offered to hire him?" von Farlenheim challenged in spite of appreciating that the second point made by the *Comtesse* would be particularly advantageous.

"He told 'Breakast' as much when they were discussing terms," Charlene explained, clearly struggling to retain her friendly tone and drumming her fingers more sharply. "And 'Breakast' is convinced he wasn't just making it up to get a higher price. Don't forget that the Council said we could rely implicitly upon his advice when hiring any assistants we require."

"I remember," the young Bosgravnian conceded, watching the movements of her fingers. He was aware that she had a violent temper and a proclivity for lashing out at anybody who antagonized her, but felt reasonably confident that she would have sufficient self-control to behave sensibly in a public place. "However, I can't recollect hearing you were authorized to pay for a task before it was completed satisfactorily."

"The decision is *mine!*" Charlene gritted out, barely able to control her asperity. Then, making an obvious effort of will, she raised the right hand in a placatory gesture and adopted a demeanour which she felt would attain the result she desired. "If necessary, when we return to report to the Council I will absolve you of all blame and take the full responsibility."

"If it becomes necessary, I wouldn't advise you to return and report," von Farlenheim answered, taking note of the woman's changed attitude and puzzled by it. Having come to know her well during their acquaintance, he realized that only something of importance could have produced such meek and conciliatory behaviour. "So I hope, for *your* sake, this man 'Clint' justifies the high opinion of his abilities."

"It appears that he does," Charlene replied, knowing the

young Bosgravnian was expressing her own thoughts on the subject. However, she had another reason for trying to win him over in addition to her awareness of the price of failure. "'Breakast' says that he not only escaped from the kind of snake in a box trap which was used to kill Walter Scargill in Brownsville, but he also survived being ambushed on the street one night. There were three men against him. He killed two and the third ran away. That suggests he is a competent gun-fighter."

"Or that he was lucky," von Farlenheim sniffed.

"*Very* lucky, if it was luck alone kept him alive," the *Comtesse* answered, refusing to be goaded. "There are few who have survived when Beguinage set out to kill them—And I've *never* heard of anybody doing it *twice*."

"*Twice*?" von Farlenheim repeated.

"Twice," Charlene confirmed. "Leaving a snake in a box to be opened by his victim was how Beguinage killed Scargill and, according to what 'Breakast' has heard, it was Beguinage who hired the three men who tried and failed to kill 'Clint.'"

"Beguinage," the Bosgravnian said pensively, disturbed by what he had been told. Then, adopting what he hoped would be an off-hand manner, he went on, "So he's here in Corpus Christie now, is he?"

"He is," Charlene declared.

Shrewdly assessing the real emotion behind von Farlenheim's attempt to sound indifferent, the *Comtesse* felt a sense of elation. It was what she had hoped to hear and she was now convinced that she could win him over to her way of thinking. Much as she hated to admit the necessity, she accepted that she must have his whole-hearted support and might even have need of his protection.

Being a very good judge of character, especially where members of the opposite sex were concerned, Charlene had been compelled to revise the opinions she had formed before sailing from Europe. It had been upon her advice that the proposed assassination of Crown Prince Rudolph was left until he arrived in the United States. She had assumed that, apart from his small retinue, his escort would consist of poorly disciplined soldiers under the command of uncouth and far from efficient officers. So the killing could be more safely and easily accomplished here than while he remained in the Old World. She was now aware that such was not the case.

Already impressed by Dusty Fog's intelligence, the *Comtesse* had found that Mark Counter and his companions were far from being the dull-witted, easily led country bumpkins she anticipated and required. None of them had struck her as potential dupes to be manipulated for her ends. So she wanted to make sure of having at least one willing ally. No matter how little regard she might have for von Farlenheim's tact and acumen, she knew him to be a man of courage and considerable skill in the use of weapons. What was more, he shared her determination to succeed in their nefarious enterprise. In fact, she was willing to concede that he had as much to gain and even more to lose from the outcome.

Although Charlene was not a native of Bosgravnia, she stood to make a considerable financial gain from the assassination. That, rather than a desire to retain near feudal rights, was her motivation. So she was ready to use any means to bring about the desired result.

A woman of great ambition, Charlene was also a realist. Knowing how much she depended upon her physical charms to make men do her bidding, she was equally aware that the attraction would not remain indefinitely. Of late, she had become increasingly aware that her skin was growing coarser. It was only slight as yet, but needed more and more attention to hide. What was more, only by being careful in her eating habits and carrying out a daily routine of exercises could she retain the magnificent figure which formed her major asset. So she was determined to establish her fortune before she lost the means to acquire it. That was why she had become an agent for the Council of Noble Birth. The reward she had been offered would be sufficient to set her up for life. Provided that she was able to earn it, of course.

The latter point was the reason for Charlene's desire to win over von Farlenheim. Beguinage's involvement was jeopardizing her chances, but it could be to the young Bosgravnian's advantage. He could achieve his own ends without danger to himself by allowing the assassin to kill the Crown Prince, but the same did not apply to her.

"Alex!" the *Comtesse* gasped, having paused to convey the

impression that a thought was just occurring to her. "Who is Beguinage working for?"

"The anarchists, of course," von Farlenheim answered. "We haven't hired him."

"*You* and I *haven't*," Charlene agreed, looking straight into the young man's face and speaking in tones of great earnest. "But if he *was* hired by the anarchists, why did he kill Scargill, who was one of them?"

"*Gott in himmel!*" von Farlenheim ejaculated, giving thought for the first time to the reason Scargill had been killed. Although not overburdened with imagination, he began to appreciate the implication behind the *Comtesse's* question. "Do you mean that he has been hired by the Council?"

"*Somebody* has hired him, he wouldn't be here otherwise," Charlene pointed out, far from dissatisfied by the response she was eliciting. "*You* haven't and *I* certainly haven't. So, if the anarchists didn't either, who else is there?"

"I can't think of *anybody*," von Farlenheim admitted, showing his puzzlement. "But why should the Council hire him after they agreed we should do it?"

"Perhaps it wasn't a *Council* decision," Charlene hinted.

"But you said—!" von Farlenheim began.

"The Council as a whole wouldn't have any need to hire him," the *Comtesse* answered. "But one of them might be acting on his own behalf."

"You mean one of them plans to have Beguinage kill the Crown Prince instead of leaving us to do it?" the Bosgravnian growled.

"*Somebody* has hired him," Charlene repeated, confident that she was establishing the required train of thought. "And whoever did would know of his reputation where anybody else who has designs upon the life of his victim is concerned. He warned me and killed Scargill as proof to both us and the anarchists that he has been hired to assassinate Rudolph and would brook no interference."

"That's true," von Farlenheim growled and anger suffused his face. "Then whoever hired Beguinage must have known that he might try to kill *us* when he found out that we had the same thing in mind."

"Perhaps that is what whoever hired him hoped he would

do, even though he wasn't told to do it," Charlene suggested, eager to press home the suspicions she had aroused as a means of ensuring von Farlenheim would support her. "So now you know why I decided to accept 'Clint's' terms."

"Huh?" the Bosgravnian grunted, frowning and showing a complete lack of understanding. "What do you mean?"

"We don't need 'Clint' to kill Rudolph," Charlene elaborated. "Our own plan will do that. But he will keep Beguinage's attention from us. And, after the way he has escaped twice, he might even—"

"What's wrong?" von Farlenheim inquired, as the woman —having glanced through the open door of the dining-room into the hotel's front lobby—stiffened slightly and stopped speaking.

"It's 'Clint!'" Charlene breathed excitedly, before she could prevent the words from being uttered. "He's at the reception desk."

A desire to see the man who had survived two attempts by Beguinage to kill him had been the *Comtesse's* reason for selecting the Portside Hotel as her rendezvous with von Farlenheim. Although she had led "Breakast" to assume that she wanted to hire "Clint" to assassinate the Crown Prince, her motives had been those which she explained to the Bosgravnian. However, she had had misgivings over having parted with six hundred dollars as an advance on the larger sum which the go-between declared "Clint" was demanding. Nor had she been enamoured of "Breakast's" refusal to let her meet the local killer personally. So she and her maid had followed the go-between when he set off to deliver the money to "Clint." She had been too far away to hear the name he mentioned to the desk clerk, but had seen the note he left placed in a pigeon-hole on the key-stand. Sending her maid to ask von Farlenheim to join her, she had picked a table in the dining-room which commanded a view of the reception desk and had waited in the hope of satisfying her curiosity.

At first, seeing that a man had arrived and was being given "Breakast's" note, Charlene had been delighted by the opportunity to impress von Farlenheim with her acumen. However, even as she was drawing the young Bosgravnian's attention to him, she began to form an uneasy impression that doing so might prove ill-advised. There was, she realized just a fraction of a second too late, something familiar about him.

Opening the note he had accepted, the newcomer turned away from the desk.

While the hair which showed from the pushed back hat and the clothing might be different from their previous meetings, Charlene was in no doubt regarding the identity of the man who was reading the message that had been awaiting the return of "*Rapido* Clint."

Nor was von Farlenheim.

"How *very* clever of you, *Comtesse*!" the young Bosgravnian hissed, his attitude reverting to the near hostility he had been exhibiting before Charlene had distracted him with her discussion of Beguinage. "You've hired *Dusty Fog*!"

CHAPTER FIVE

You Could've Got Me Killed

Faced with what appeared to be an attempt upon his life, Crown Prince Rudolph of Bosgravnia was unable to control an involuntary and instinctive reaction which caused him to step backwards. With his retreating foot missing the trunk of the tree upon which he was standing, he lost his balance. Even as he was starting to fall, his eyes were registering a comprehensive description of the person who was responsible for his predicament.

Writing about the incident later, the Crown Prince would comment upon how amazed he was at the amount of detail the human mind was capable of absorbing in a fleeting instant and despite being under considerable stress.[1]

Slightly over six foot tall and possessing a powerful physique that had not yet filled out to full manhood, the cause of Rudolph's sense of alarm was a blond-haired youngster whose pleasantly handsome features hardly seemed to accord with his apparently hostile actions. His Texas-style black J.B. Stetson hat, having been dislodged by the speed with which he was moving, had slipped backwards as he was springing from his place of concealment, and dangled by its fancy *barbiquejo* chinstrap on the shoulders of a brown and white calfskin vest. Tightly rolled, a flaming red bandana trailed its long ends over the front of an open-necked dark green shirt. The legs of his well-worn Levi's pants hung outside tan-coloured boots of the kind the royal visitor would come to know were peculiar to

---

1. This point came to light when Alvin Dustine "Cap" Fog found a copy of Crown Prince Rudolph's book JAGDERLEBNISSE IN TEXAS (*Hunting Experiences in Texas*) and gave the author permission to make use of the information it contained.—*J.T.E.*

working cowhands.[2] The brown leather of the *buscadero* gunbelt from the tied down holsters of which he was drawing a
pair of staghorn-handled Colt 1860 Army revolvers had
clearly been cut and shaped by a master craftsman.

Subconsciously taking in the particulars of his apparent assailant's appearance while tumbling backwards, Rudolph began
to wonder if his apprehensions might be baseless. Moving with a
speed that he could barely believe was possible, the seven-and-
a-half-inch-long "Civilian" pattern barrels[3] of the youngster's
weapons were turning into alignment as soon as they cleared the
lips of the holsters. Just as they roared, practically simultaneously and in about a second from the first movements of their
owner's hands towards the butts, the Crown Prince realized that
they were pointing downwards and had not been elevated sufficiently to endanger him. There was further evidence to support
his supposition, but the youngster had passed beneath his range
of vision before he could notice it.

On the point of accepting Mark Counter's offer of help to
climb over the tree after Rudolph, the beautiful young Englishwoman stared at the blond youngster. The gasp she gave was one
of surprise and alarm rather than fright. Rising swiftly, her right
hand disappeared into the outside pocket of her jacket and closed
upon something. However, before she could bring out whatever
she was grasping, she halted the movement. It was becoming
obvious that in spite of appearances, no assassination bid had
been intended by the newcomer.

Having fired, the youngster brought his hands upwards and
extended his arms as in a gesture of surrender. Furthermore,
as the Colts were being raised, he twirled them upon his trigger fingers so that the barrels pointed at the ground and he

2. The sharp toes of a cowhand's boots were an aid to slipping into and
out of a stirrup iron hurriedly when necessary and the high heels could be
spiked into the ground for greater security when roping on foot.—*J.T.E.*
3. Colt 1860 Army revolvers which were manufactured to fulfil military
contracts had eight-inch-long barrels. An explanation of the term "Army" is
given for the benefit of new readers in Footnote 16, Appendix One.—*J.T.E.*

grasped them by the cylinders in such a fashion that he would be unable to shoot.

Because Colonel Wilhelm Liebenfrau and Major the Baron von Goeringwald were following some yards behind the Crown Prince's party, their view was impeded by the Lady and the blond giant. So they could only see part of what was happening. Thinking that their ruler had been shot, the Personal Attendant spat out a furious oath in Bosgravnian. Sending his right hand to the hilt of the sabre, he changed his marching gait into a lumbering run.

Equally alarmed by the possibility of a successful assassination, the *aide-de-camp* grabbed at the closed flap of his awkwardly positioned holster. Instantly, he discovered the disadvantages of such a rig which had been obvious to Mark when he had referred to it earlier. Fumbling in his haste, he found difficulty in even freeing the flap from its retaining pin as he sprang forward on the Colonel's heels to help avenge the attack upon their royal master.

Hearing the shots from the position at the head of the small advance guard, Captain Fritz von Farlenheim spun around. To his consternation, he discovered that the rest of the party was out of sight beyond the bend in the trail he had just turned. Concern for the Crown Prince's welfare led him to act impulsively and without considering the consequences. The three sailors who were accompanying him were also turning. Although each was carrying a loaded Springfield single-shot carbine more readily accessible than his revolver, he shoved between them as he went back to investigate. Nor was he any more successful than von Goeringwald in drawing the weapon.

By the time the First Taster came into view of the tree, with the sailors running on his heels, his revolver was still held in the grip of the holster. In spite of the youngster raising the Colts in a way that showed he did not mean to use them again, von Farlenheim continued to advance, trying to extract his weapon at the same time. Before he could achieve the latter, he was confronted by a man who bounded swiftly from behind a bush at the left side of the trail.

Slightly shorter than the blond youngster and with a more slender, yet wiry, build, the newcomer was clad from head to foot in all black cowhand-style garments. However, while the toes were pointed, his boots had low heels which would make them more comfortable when walking. The sombre hue of his attire was relieved only by the brown walnut handle of an old Colt Second Model Dragoon revolver which rode butt forward in a low cavalry-twist holster on the right side of his belt, and the concave ivory hilt of an enormous James Black bowie knife sheathed at the left. His hair was as black as the wing of the crow and his handsome face as dark as that of an Indian. However, in spite of the latter having an aspect of almost babyishly innocent youth, there was something in his red hazel eyes that suggested he was older than he looked, and not a man with whom it would be wise, or safe, to trifle. Carrying a Winchester Model of 1866 rifle, he handled it with the deft ease of one well versed in its use.

Although taken just as unawares as the rest of the party by the young cowhand's appearance and actions, Mark Counter reacted with commendable rapidity. Shooting forward his hands, he caught the Crown Prince under the armpits. It was testimony to his enormous strength that he had no difficulty in averting what could otherwise have been a serious fall.

What was more, drawing an accurate conclusion from the sounds which arose behind him, the blond giant did not merely lower his burden to the ground. Instead, apparently without any more effort than if he was holding a newly born baby rather than a grown man, he swung around so that Liebenfrau and von Goeringwald could see their ruler was unharmed. In passing, he noticed how the Lady was standing and was impressed by her composure. There was neither fear nor panic in her face, only an expression of grim determination and her posture suggested that she might be about to draw a weapon of some kind from the jacket pocket.

"It's all right, Colonel!" Mark stated, setting Rudolph down on his feet and having more urgent matters demanding his attention than considering the Englishwoman's behaviour. "He's one of my men!"

"Hold hard there, you-all!" the black dressed young man was commanding while the blond giant was speaking, swinging his rifle at waist level so that its muzzle menaced first von Farlenheim and then the three sailors. "I don't know why the boy cut loose, but it wasn't to harm your—"

Paying no attention to the words and ignoring the evidence which suggested they were the truth, the First Taster stopped trying to liberate his revolver. Giving no thought to the fact that the speaker was armed with a weapon which could be fired with great rapidity when in such competent hands, or how it would be unlikely to miss at so short a range, he sprang onwards. It was his intention to grapple with the black dressed man, even if doing so cost him his life. It was a brave, but unwise action and could have cost him dearly.

Taking a swift pace to meet the advancing Bosgravnian, the Indian dark newcomer deftly kept the rifle clear of his grabbing hands and thrust forward with it. The barrel caught von Farlenheim in the *solar plexus* with sufficient force to rob him of his breath and folded him at the waist like a closing jack-knife. Stepping aside while delivering the jab, his assailant let him collapse to his knees and returned the Winchester to its previous alignment before any of the sailors could try to profit from his diversion.

"Don't try it!" the black dressed man warned, his lazy-sounding Texas drawl charged with menace and his face losing all its babyish innocence, as one of the trio made as if to raise his carbine.

"Hell, no, *don't*!" yelped the seaman who had identified the blond giant as the U.S.S. *Nantucket's* barge was approaching the beach, swinging his left hand to thrust down his companion's weapon. "That's the Ysabel Kid and he works for Ole Devil Hardin same's Mark Counter."

Unlike his Texas-born shipmate, the first sailor had never heard of the Ysabel Kid.[4] For all that, the warning had not been entirely necessary. He had already began to suspect that his aggression might be ill-advised and likely to put his life in jeopardy. Not only had the Winchester turned in his direction with disconcerting steadiness, there was a coldly savage look about its owner that reminded him of paintings he had seen depicting Indian warriors on the warpath. So, following his

4. For the benefit of new readers, details of the Ysabel Kid's background and special qualifications are recorded in Appendix Three.—*J.T.E.*

companions' example, he stopped and allowed the Springfield to remain pointing at the ground.

"Why the shooting, Waco?" Mark inquired, after having turned from the three Bosgravnians and satisfied himself that, like them, the advance party would not be taking any hostile action.

"That first bunch to come over the tree must've disturbed a big old copperhead," the blond youngster answered, his accent showing that he too was a son of the Lone Star State, bringing down and twirling away the Colts almost as rapidly as he had drawn and fired them. "He was coming out this side and, happen that gent'd jumped down so near, was likely to have riled up enough to chomp him on the leg."

"A *copperhead*?" Liebenfrau growled, coming to a halt and thrusting back his half-drawn sabre. "And what might *that* be, Mr. Counter?"

"Just about the most dangerous kind of poisonous snake we have down here, Colonel," the blond giant replied, but refrained from explaining how the species *Ancistrodon Mokasen* was more feared than any of the rattlesnake family because of its almost silent mode of attack and speed when striking. He pointed in the direction from which they had come, where shouts of alarm were sounding from the beach beyond the trees. "We'd best let them know there's no cause for alarm."

"Go and tell them, Baron," the Personal Attendant ordered and, as the *aide-de-camp* returned along the trail, glanced to where the Crown Prince was climbing over the log. Then he brought his attention back to Mark and his voice was somewhat less harsh than usual as he continued, "I think an explanation is necessary."

"And me," the big blond agreed, then looked at the Englishwoman. "Can I help you over, ma'am?"

"Thank you," the Lady answered, having removed her empty hand from the pocket. "Provided the snake isn't still able to—chomp—anybody, I think the term is."

"It's dead, Freddie," Rudolph declared, turning his gaze from the torn apart body of the large snake to the cause of it's death. "I'm in your debt, my capable young friend. If you'd called a warning, or moved less quickly, I would not have been able to stop myself jumping down."

"I sort of figured it out that way myself," the youngster admitted.

"But leaping out and acting as you did could have put your own life at risk," the Crown Prince pointed out.

"I thought some about *that* as well," the youngster declared, then looked over his shoulder and his voice took on a note of asperity as he raised it. "Showing these good folks how quiet 'n' sneaky we can move was one right smart notion, Lon. Why damn it, you could've got me killed."

"I *could've*, but not with the way my luck's been running so bad these days," the black dressed young man answered, showing no suggestion of remorse over having put a good friend's life in danger. Swinging his gaze to von Farlenheim, who was glaring up at him furiously and starting to rise, he extended his right hand and continued, "I'm right sorry I had to rough handle you-all that ways, mister. Only I could see's you wasn't fixing to believe what I'd told you and there wasn't going to be time to talk it out peaceable."

"Captain von Farlenheim!" Leibenfrau barked, as the young Bosgravnian thrust himself erect without assistance.

"Yes, sir?" the First Taster answered, snapping into a brace and facing the speaker instead of carrying out his intention of striking the Indian-dark Texan.

"Send your men back to the beach," the Personal Attendant ordered, following the Crown Prince over the tree with an agility many a younger man would have been hard put to better. Waiting until Mark had helped the Lady across the trunk, he went on, "And now, Mr. Counter—"

"I think that the explanation can wait until after we've been introduced, Colonel," Rudolph interrupted. "Am I correct in assuming these gentlemen are part of our escort, Mr. Counter?"

"They're part of it, but the 'gentlemen' part is debatable," Mark replied and indicated the youngster with what might have been considered a derisory wave of his left hand. "He's Waco."

"Just 'Waco?'" the Crown Prince inquired, when the introduction was not extended beyond the one name.

"'Just' just about sums him up," Mark drawled.

"He gets called plenty of other things, though," the Indian-dark Texan commented, strolling over followed by a clearly angry von Farlenheim. His admiring gaze flickered to the Englishwoman as he concluded, "Only we don't use such language afore ladies, deacons or children."

"He'll likely try to tell you his name's Loncey Dalton Ysabel, ma'am," the youngster whose only name was Waco[5] informed the Lady. "But he's better known, or worse, as the Ysabel Kid. Don't let that, or how he looks fool you. He's older 'n' more ornery—"

"You keep your lips together," the blond giant ordered, but his attitude was that of an older brother addressing a favourite sibling. "Unless you-all want to tell us what kind of fool game you pair've been playing at."

"It was all Lon's fault's usual," Waco protested, jerking a thumb in a gesture filled with contempt at the Ysabel Kid. "He's full of right smart notions. Trouble being, he only turns loose the bad ones."

Carrying on, the youngster confirmed the theory Mark had already formed over what had happened. Listening from the concealment of the woodland after the Crown Prince and his retinue had landed from the *Nantucket's* barge, the two OD Connected cowhands had heard the doubts which were raised about their competence as his bodyguard. So the Kid had suggested that they gave an exhibition of their ability to move silently and undetected close by while the party were walking to the Coast Road. Keeping slightly ahead of Rudolph's portion of the party, Waco had seen the danger and had acted in the only way he could. Realizing how the youngster's behaviour might be misinterpreted, the Kid had taken measures to prevent harm befalling him before he could explain what he was doing.

"Which I should've known a heap better'n do any fool thing *he* suggested," Waco concluded, aiming a glare of well simulated disdain at his Indian-dark *amigo*. "All doing it proved's that we're sneaky and, looking at him, nobody needs to have *that* proved."

"You proved more than *that*," Rudolph objected. "I've

5. Waco's background and qualifications are given in Appendix Four.—
J.T.E.

never seen anybody who could draw one revolver so quickly, much less two, then shoot with such accuracy."

"Shucks," Waco replied, flushing a little. "I wasn't figuring on *hitting* the snake when I cut loose. All I did was throw lead down there and hope it'd make you jump backwards instead of down this side of the tree."

"He can't shoot worth a cuss," the Kid stated. "And, way he was stumping around, I figured you'd hear him for sure."

"I never saw or heard either of you," the Crown Prince objected. "Did you, Colonel?"

"No, Your Highness," Liebenfrau answered and directed a sour scowl at von Farlenheim who was approaching with the three sailors. "Nor did *anybody* else!"

"It's not real likely any of them heard or saw us, Colonel," the Kid drawled. "I learned that kind of sneaky moving from the *Pehnane* Comanche, which there don't come any better. And *I've* taught Waco *all* he knows."

"Only about sneaky moving," the youngster supplemented, addressing the words to the Lady. "He's not a whole heap of use for anything—"

"And that makes two of you," Mark interrupted, eyeing Waco in a threatening manner, then starting to perform the introductions.

As had been the case when Rudolph had first spoken to the blond giant, he found the demeanour of the other two Texans equally unexceptionable. Furthermore, he considered that the way in which Waco particularly had coped with the potentially dangerous situation suggested they were well able to act as his protectors. Not only had the youngster reached the correct solution over how to deal with the snake very quickly, he had also realized that he must demonstrate his lack of hostile intentions when he had done so. That he had taken such a risk implied a complete faith in the Ysabel Kid being able to protect him from the advance guard until the position was explained. What was more, in spite of the sardonic comments which passed between them and the blond giant, it was obvious that there were very close bonds of friendship and loyalty among them.

Nor, the Crown Prince decided, could the two young Texans' behaviour be faulted when they were being introduced to Liebenfrau and von Farlenheim. There was nothing self

conscious or deliberately brash in either's manner. It was clear
that they respected the Colonel and neither showed any resentment or concern over the First Taster's stiff-backed and
obvious disapproval.

"And this's Lady Winifred Amelia Besgrove-Woodstole,"
Mark concluded, indicating the Englishwoman who had
waited in the background until the presentations of the Bosgravnian party were made.

"Lady Wini—!" Waco began, losing his smile and snapping his eyes around to look briefly at the Kid. Then, swinging an interrogative gaze to Mark, he received a negative
shake of the head. Turning his attention back to the Lady, he
no longer displayed his earlier admiration and his voice became almost defensive in its neutrally polite timbre as he went
on, "I'm pleased to meet you-all, ma'am."

"It's a right honour to make your acquaintance, ma'am," the
Kid continued, but his even tone held no suggestion of friendli-
ness and his Indian-dark features were devoid of any expression.
"We don't often meet a for real lady out this ways."

"Well now, seeing's we all know each other, how about us
moving on over to the Coast Road?" Mark inquired, giving no
hint as to what could have caused his companions' response to
the introduction. "The quicker we get you gents into cowhand
clothes, the earlier we'll have you-all into Corpus Christie."

Although none of the Bosgravnians appeared to have noticed the change in the Texans' attitudes, the Lady was more
perceptive and felt disquieted. She had already sensed that
something about her was disturbing the blond giant, but had
thought it to be no more than an objection to having had the
added responsibility of her presence forced upon him without
prior warning. If that was the case, neither of his companions
had been sharing his sentiments. It was not until they heard
her name that they had changed their way of thinking where
she was concerned. In which case, unlikely as the explanation
which sprang most readily to mind might seem, she knew that
she could find herself in a difficult situation.

CHAPTER SIX

We Will Pay You More

For a few seconds after he had delivered his mocking comment, Alex von Farlenheim wondered if he had pushed Charlene, *Comtesse de* Petain too far. Never had he seen a human countenance display such concentrated venomous rage as that which twisted at her beautiful features. If looks could have killed, the glare she directed at him as her right hand closed almost spasmodically around the fan on the table would have tumbled him lifeless to the floor. Alarmed, he tensed ready to defend himself if she struck at him with the device she had grabbed.

However, despite being a-quiver with fury, Charlene had sufficient strength of will and intelligence to prevent herself from acting in a manner which would attract unwanted attention. Promising herself that she would be avenged upon the young Bosgravnian once he had served his purpose, she concentrated upon regaining her composure. What she discovered as she glanced at the dining-room's door warned that there was an urgent need for her to do so. Forcing herself to smile, she raised her right hand in what could have passed as a friendly wave.

"*He's* seen us and is coming over!" the *Comtesse* warned, losing the smile briefly as she turned her gaze to von Farlenheim and gritting out the words *sotto voce*. "So, whatever you do, be very *careful* in how you act, and think first about all you say."

Having finished reading the note left by "George Breakast," informing him that his terms had been accepted and arranging a rendezvous if they did not meet at the Edgehurst Warehouse, Dusty Fog had commenced what was purely a precautionary glance around the lobby of the Portside Hotel. Seeing the couple in the dining-room, he had guessed what brought them there and had felt sure that they had not come with the go-between's knowledge or approval. Their attitudes, when his gaze first reached them, supplied a clue as to how the discovery of "*Rapido* Clint's" real identity was being received. So, even before the *Comtesse* had made the pretence of having just become aware of his presence, he had decided what to do.

Thrusting the note into his trousers' pocket, the small Texan strolled towards the couple. He noticed that Charlene was the more composed of the two. While she was managing to smile as she watched him approaching, von Farlenheim scowled and moved restlessly. Dusty considered that, of the two, the young Bosgravnian was the more likely to make some damaging statement if handled in the proper manner. He was equally aware that the woman would do everything in her power to prevent it from happening.

"Why howdy, *Comtesse*, Mr. von Farlenheim," the small Texan greeted, removing his hat and coming to a halt at the table.

"Good morning, Captain Fog," Charlene replied, proving just as adept at speaking English as she had while employing German. "This *is* a surprise. We had no idea that you were in Corpus Christie. But, if the change to the colour of your hair means what I think it does, that is hardly surprising. Won't you join us?"

"Why thank you 'most to death, ma'am," Dusty drawled, having hoped for the invitation. Giving no sign of noticing von Farlenheim's baleful glare, he hung his Stetson by its *barbiquejo* on the back of the chair he drew out. Then, acting as if the Bosgravnian was not there, he sat down and continued to address the woman, "And what do *you-all* think the change means, ma'am?"

"That the telegraph message you were supposed to have received from your uncle was a fake," Charlene answered, flickering a look at von Farlenheim as he stirred in irritation over the Texan's treatment. "You pretended you had been called home so that you could leave Brownsville with your appearance changed and come to find out if there is any danger here to Rud—His Highness."

"You're close to calling it right, ma'am," Dusty declared,

knowing that the amendment in the *Comtesse's* way of referring to the royal visitor had been made as a reminder that she
was on very good terms with him.

"Only *close*?" Charlene asked, pouting in a way which she
knew made her look puzzled and, by appealing to the masculine ego, generally produced either information or some other
service that she required from the man she was addressing.

"Shucks, I didn't need to come here to find out if there was
going to be any danger, ma'am," Dusty elaborated, mentally
conceding that the woman knew how to utilize her physical
attractions to their best advantage. He felt sure she had employed them against the other members of the floating outfit,
but was confident that none would have succumbed. "I *knew*
that there would be. So, seeing's how that Beguinage
hombre's the biggest danger of all, I came here acting like a
hired killer hunting work to see if I could smoke him out."

"Good heavens!" Charlene gasped, guessing what the term
implied although she had never heard it used in such a context. Her hand fluttered up to her throat in well simulated
alarm and she went on, "You mean that, in spite of knowing
he had killed others with the same intention, you deliberately
allowed Beguinage to believe you would be willing to kill
Rud—His Highness?"

"It seemed like the only thing to do," Dusty confirmed,
still ignoring von Farlenheim's presence at the table.

"But how gallant and courageous of you!" the *Comtesse*
praised, changing her attitude to one of wide-eyed admiration.
Although she doubted whether the small Texan came into such
a category, especially after her lack of success where his three
companions were concerned, she continued to employ tactics
which had lured more than one impressionable young man—
and some who should have been old enough to know better—
into her clutches. "I hope that your brave and noble
endeavours have been rewarded with the success they de-
serve."

"There's some who'd claim they have," Dusty answered,
adopting an air of blatantly false modesty which he felt sure
would annoy von Farlenheim. "Fact being, Beguinage'll not
be killing anybody else."

"Do you mean that you have captured him *already*?" Charlene gasped, genuinely impressed by the thought.

So was von Farlenheim, in spite of his resentment over the way in which the small Texan was treating him. Like the *Comtesse*, he was aware that every law enforcement agency in Europe had tried in vain to apprehend the assassin and none had even achieved as much as learning his identity.

"No, ma'am, not *captured*," Dusty corrected, without giving as much as a glance to the other occupant of the table. "Way things turned out, I had to shoot him."

"Shoot him?" von Farlenheim barked, unable to restrain himself any longer. He remembered his uncle's comments regarding the small Texan's abilities where handling firearms were concerned. "So he is dead then!"

"I've never seen anybody wind up deader," Dusty replied, deciding that the time had come for him to start trying to profit from his treatment of the young Bosgravnian. "Not even that jasper from up north who offered me two hundred and fifty dollars to gun the Prince down."

"*Two hundred and fif*—!" von Farlenheim commenced heatedly, swinging a glare of accusation at the *Comtesse*.

"I *agree*, Alex!" Charlene said, in a purr that was charged with a furious warning when taken in conjunction with the savage glare she turned upon him, before he could continue. "That *does* seem a paltry sum for agreeing to assassinate such an important person—Not that I know anything about such things, of course." Then, looking as if the thought had just struck her, she returned her attention to the small Texan and set about diverting his thoughts from the Bosgravnian's potential gaffe, "But are you *sure* the man was serious, Captain Fog?"

"Why else would he have come to me, ma'am?" Dusty inquired, showing nothing to suggest he had drawn any conclusions from von Farlenheim's comment.

"Perhaps he was nothing more than a somewhat foolish young man who hoped to be able to tell his friends that he had met a famous—hired killer, I think you called yourself."

"That's what I made folks think I was," Dusty conceded. "But, happen that was *all* there was to it, he paid a high price for doing it."

"A *very* high price," the *Comtesse* agreed, throwing another prohibitive frown at von Farlenheim. Looking back at the Texan, she continued, "Why did you kill him?"

"I didn't," Dusty corrected, watching the Bosgravnian swing a startled and worried glance at the woman.

"But you implied that he had to be—!" Charlene protested, bringing the words to a halt as a waiter who had entered arrived at the table. She sounded just a trifle relieved as she went on, "I'm afraid we've already eaten, Captain Fog. But if you would care to take something—?"

"Nothing for me, ma'am, *gracias*," Dusty drawled, realizing to his annoyance that the interruption was allowing the Bosgravnian to recover his composure.

"You may bring our account," Charlene informed the waiter and, after he had withdrawn, turned back to the Texan. "Isn't he dead, then?"

"He's dead all right," Dusty admitted, deciding that there was little chance of eliciting any guilty admissions from the pair. He might have succeeded with von Farlenheim if he could have kept the conversation along the lines it had been taking, but the arrival of the waiter had broken it, and Charlene would make sure that it did not return to such a dangerous level. "But I didn't kill him. The town marshal had heard he was a hired gun from up North, figured he might be after one of us, and shot him before I could stop it."

"How *unfortunate*," the *Comtesse* declared, sounding so solicitous that the sentiment might have been genuine. Noticing that von Farlenheim was making no attempt to conceal his relief at learning there was no danger of the go-between betraying them, she concluded it would be wise to remove him from the small Texan's presence. She had already deduced that Dusty was hoping to provoke him into some incriminating comment and had managed to prevent it happening so far. Her gaze went to the clock on the wall and she gasped, "Good heavens. Is that the time? We must go and greet His Highness when he disembarks, Alex."

"There's no rush, ma'am," Dusty drawled, as von Farlenheim followed the *Comtesse's* example and started to rise. "He's not coming in on that steam-sloop."

"I don't understand," Charlene replied, continuing to stand up.

"He and his party've been landed along the coast a ways," the small Texan explained. "Mark and the boys're waiting there and will be fetching him in later today."

"You're a much more clever man than I thought, Captain Fog," the *Comtesse* stated truthfully, although she was writhing inwardly at the latest evidence of how she had been outwitted. "I'm delighted to find out that Rud—the Crown Prince's welfare is in such capable hands, aren't you, Alex?"

"Yes!" von Farlenheim barked, the word leaving his mouth like the cork popping from a bottle of champagne.

"So much excitement!" Charlene gasped, fanning herself with the empty left hand and picking up the fan in the right. "I feel that I must have a breath of fresh air to revive me. Let's take a stroll, Alex."

"Yes," the Bosgravnian acceded, wanting an opportunity to speak with his fellow-conspirator privately.

"Perhaps you would care to accompany us, Captain Fog?" Charlene suggested, making the invitation sound genuine although she hoped it would be refused so she would be free to deal with von Farlenheim.

"I'd admire to, ma'am," Dusty replied, appearing equally sincere. "But I'm figuring on getting my hair back to its real colour before the reception tonight."

"His Highness will be here in time for it?" the *Comtesse* asked.

"Why sure," Dusty confirmed. "One thing you can say about those boys of mine, they *always* follow orders. Which's why Mark didn't tell you the truth about where he was going, ma'am. I hope you-all don't hold it against him, but he'd been told to keep it to himself."

"That was quite correct," Charlene declared, guessing the comment had been made to provoke either herself or von Farlenheim into a protest. She wondered what other orders Mark Counter had been given with regard to herself, but was consoled by the thought that she had neither done nor said anything to suggest her involvement in the plot against the Crown Prince. "You may tell him that I understand. We will see you at the reception?"

"You can count on it, ma'am," Dusty answered, standing and lifting his hat from the back of the chair. Watching the couple walk away as he was donning it, he grinned and thought, "Now *that's* given you both something to think about, I'd reckon. And, lady, you're going to have to do some right fancy explaining to him, the way things have gone wrong for you."

Despite his conclusions, the small Texan knew he had not removed the couple as a threat to the life of the Crown Prince. While he felt sure that they were involved, "Breakast's" death had ruined one way by which he could have gained evidence of their complicity. The conversation that had just taken place had also failed to produce any proof. Nor could he now hope to gain it by means of Mark's association with Charlene after what had been said. In fact, the discovery she had made would make her even more wary and hard to trap.

Unlike many men of his age and period, Dusty had no sense of masculine supremacy. He realized that he was up against an intelligent, unscrupulous and dangerous antagonist in the *Comtesse de* Petain. Thinking of other members of her sex against whom he had found himself in contention over the years, he did not consider the fact that she was a woman made her any the less deadly. Rather the opposite, as she was an expert in turning her physical attributes to good advantage. He wished he had another of her gender to help him by meeting her at her own level.

Wondering if he should try to obtain the services of Belle Boyd, or even his cousin Betty Hardin, Dusty strolled from the dining-room. From what he had been told, he knew that the Rebel Spy was engaged upon a mission in her capacity as a member of the United States' Secret Service and would be unavailable.[1] Deciding he would ask the Crown Prince if his cousin could join the hunting party, should Charlene contrive to be included in it, he went towards the stairs which led to the guests' rooms. He had told the truth to the couple about his intentions. With Beguinage and "Breakast" dead, particularly as the *Comtesse* and von Farlenheim were aware of "*Rapido*

1. New readers can find details of Belle Boyd's connection with Dusty Fog in Appendix One. What the mission was is told in: THE REMITTANCE KID *and* WHIP AND THE WAR LANCE.—*J.T.E.*

Clint's" true identity, there was no point in continuing the deception. So he wanted to return to his normal appearance before attending the reception.

A thickset man of slightly over middle height was standing at the foot of the stairs and looking upwards. He was clad in the kind of dark blue peaked cap, semi-uniform pea-jacket, with black trousers tucked into heavy sea boots, frequently worn by officers of merchant ships. Both hands were thrust into the jacket's pockets. In spite of that, beyond noticing he had a hard Slavic face partially obscured by a neatly-trimmed grizzled black beard, Dusty paid little attention to him in passing. Captains and mates of cargo or passenger vessels were not an unusual sight at the Portside Hotel.

"Mr. Clint," the man said, speaking in a low voice as the small Texan started to ascend the stairs. His English had a guttural timbre, but little trace of an accent.

"If you-all're meaning me, mister," Dusty replied, just as quietly, halting and looking over his shoulder. "You've got the wrong name."

"It is the one given to me by the bartender at the Binnacle Tavern," the man answered, and twisted his head to glance in the direction of the main entrance, through which Charlene and von Farlenheim could be seen crossing the street. "But if I do have the wrong man, I apologize."

"And if you haven't?" Dusty challenged, knowing that the bartender worked for Rameses Turtle and had been instructed to send any potential employers to see him at the hotel.

"I have a proposition which may be of interest to you," the man replied, without removing his hands from the pockets.

"Could be I'm already hired," Dusty warned, turning to face the man and hooking his thumbs in his gunbelt.

"If you are," the man said, throwing another look and a nod towards the front door, "whatever they are offering you, we will pay you more to work for us."

"Sounds like you and me'd best do some talking," Dusty suggested. Although the *Comtesse* and the Bosgravnian had disappeared from view, the man's gesture had been sufficiently informative for him to decide that continuing the conversation could be worthwhile. "Only I don't reckon's this's the place to do it. We'd best go on up to my room."

"I would prefer somewhere more public," the man stated, a wary glint coming to his eyes. "Just as a precaution, you understand."

"Why sure," Dusty conceded, in an off-hand manner. "One thing I admire is a cautious *hombre*. Fact being, I'm a mite that way myself. So you'd best let go of that gun and bring your hands out empty."

"Wh—?" the man began.

"Do it!" Dusty ordered and, despite his voice retaining its even tone, there was something subtly differing about his bearing. "I can draw, shoot and kill you before you can turn it into line."

Stiffening slightly, the man stared at the *big* Texan for a few seconds. Like the town marshal, he was so impressed by the strength of Dusty's personality that he no longer thought in mere feet and inches where his challenger was concerned. Nor did he doubt that the other was confident of being able to carry out the statement. Slowly, hesitantly, he opened his fingers to release the butt of the Colt Storekeeper Model Peacemaker in the right side pocket and brought his hands into view.

"That's better," Dusty drawled, glancing around to make sure they were not attracting attention. "Would the bar over there be public enough for you?"

"It will," the man agreed, impressed by what had happened.

For all that the desk clerk had noticed, the two might have merely met in an amicable fashion. Apart from glancing up as they made their way towards the bar-room, he paid no attention to them.

Following the man in, Dusty took the lead and picked a table which commanded a view of the street through the window. There were only a few customers and none close enough to overhear a conversation if it was carried out with circumspection. A waiter came over to take their order as they sat down.

"All right now, mister, let's get the deck dealt and see how the cards fall," Dusty requested, after the drinks had been delivered and the waiter had returned to the counter. "First one up being, what do I call you?"

"You mean my *name*?" the man asked, looking uneasy.

"Happen you-all want to give it to me," Dusty replied, his whole attitude implying disinterest. "If not, you can tie on any fancy brand you've a mind to for me to use."

"Call me— 'Gotz,'" the man offered.

"Why sure, Mr.—'Gotz,'" Dusty accepted cheerfully. "Second card's come up. It's why do you-all want to hire me."

"To kill the tyrant—!" "Gotz" began, raising his voice slightly.

"Don't tell the whole damned room," Dusty growled. "Anyways, that's what your bunch brought in good old 'Sharpshooter' Schindler to do."

"Don't play games with me, Mr. Cl—!" "Gotz" commenced.

"Keep your voice down, damn you!" Dusty interrupted in a hiss charged with menace.

"Schindler is dead, as *you* know!" the man pointed out, but in a much lower key than his previous pair of utterances. "I heard the marshal saying so at the warehouse. Did you kill both him and Beguinage?"

"I would have, but Beguinage got to him first," Dusty answered. Although he realized that his true identity had not been revealed as he had requested, he did not know what else Marshal Digbry might have said. So he decided against claiming responsibility for Schindler's death. "You see, Mr. 'Gotz,' I'm like Beguinage. I don't take to long-horns coming in and trying to graze my range, happen you know what I mean."

"I do," the man admitted, as impressed as the *Comtesse* and von Farlenheim had been by the knowledge that the Texan had succeeded in killing Europe's "premier assassin."

"Then my question still goes, 'cept I'll put it another way," Dusty continued. "Why're *you* so all fired eager to pay me as much as I'm going to ask for killing the Crown Prince when all you have to do is sit back and let them hire me to do it? He'd be just as dead and it won't cost you-all a thin dime."

"The difference, Mr. Clint," "Gotz" said, employing a dramatic near whisper. "Is that we want you to *kill* the tyrant."

"And they *don't*?" Dusty inquired, adopting a similar tone.

"They have their own plan, intended to make it appear that

we are responsible," the man explained. "All they wanted from you was that you kept Beguinage occupied. Now he is dead, they have no further need for you."

"Seemed right eager to keep me on just now, though," Dusty remarked. "And I'd told them about me burning Beguinage down."

"They'd hardly be likely to tell you the truth," "Gotz" pointed out. "But I can assure you that they were only using you to act as a lure for him and never meant to let you earn that sum you asked for by killing the tyrant."

"Sounds like you've got somebody close to them, learning what they're up to," Dusty suggested and raised a prohibitive hand. "Don't bother denying it. That's your affair and I'd reckon you'd be *loco* if you hadn't. So, seeing's you know how much I was to get, let's hear you raise the ante."

"I don't understand."

"How much higher'll you-all pay?"

"*Higher*?" "Gotz" repeated. "But I just told you that they didn't intend to let you earn the sum—"

"You also told me that *you* did," Dusty reminded the man. "Which I'd not take any less for doing it. But, just to show you my heart's in the right place, I'll not ask for any *more*. Take it or leave it, mister. Because that's the only deal you'll get from me. Bring on the four thousand dollars—"

"*Four* thousand!" "Gotz" spat out indignantly. "*They* were only offering three thousand five hundred!"

"Well I swan, so they were!" Dusty ejaculated, in tones of mock exasperation, having satisfied himself that the anarchists had a very close source of information to the aristocrats' plans. "I must be getting old, forgetting a thing like that. Like I said, just to show my heart's in the right place, I'll take the chore for three thousand five hundred."

"That's a lot of money," "Gotz" objected. "I don't know whether we can—"

"Then find out," Dusty ordered, starting to shove back his chair. "Tell your *amigos* I'll throw in the lady and that bownecked *hombre* who's with her to boot."

"To *boot*?" "Gotz" queried, looking puzzled.

"That's trading talk for something tossed in free at the end of a deal," the small Texan explained, standing up. "Well, is it a go?"

"I'll have to speak with my comrades," the bearded man replied, also rising.

"Don't take too long, and I'll have a couple of hundred as a retainer," Dusty drawled. "That buys you the chance to dicker later and stops me telling *them* you're doing it."

"Very well," "Gotz" growled, taking out a wallet and counting money from it. "Can I communicate with you here?"

"Why sure," Dusty agreed, knowing he had left the anarchist no other choice but to make the "advance payment" and confident it would produce results. "If I'm not around, leave a letter with the desk clerk. Only don't take too long in coming back."

"I won't," "Gotz" promised and turned to walk away.

"Well, '*Rapido* Clint,' you ornery son-of-a-bitch," Dusty mused, shoving back his hat to run fingers through the black hair. "It looks like you're going to have to stay alive a mite longer after all."

CHAPTER SEVEN

Only He and the Corpse Were Present

Although Dusty Fog had come face to face with many unpleasant sights in the course of his event-filled young life, the discovery he made shortly after sundown at the building which housed the town marshal's office came as sufficient of a shock to bring him to a halt.

The small Texan had intended to try to follow the anarchist called "Gotz" and find out with whom he was working, but he had been prevented from doing so. Just before he entered the lobby, he had seen two men who he had met elsewhere in connection with the cattle business. So he had been compelled to stay out of their sight in case they should recognize him and address him by his name, or comment upon his changed appearance. When he was able to leave the Portside Hotel, "Gotz" was no longer in view.

Instead of wasting time in what he had suspected would have been a futile attempt at discovering where the anarchist had gone, Dusty had made his way to the Binnacle Tavern. The information he had obtained there regarding "Gotz" left him a little wiser than he had been prior to his arrival. The bartender had told the anarchist where "*Rapido* Clint" was staying, supplied the name with which he had signed the hotel's register and described him, but had not tried to find out how or where the inquirer could be contacted.

Listening to various comments from the other customers about the events at the Edgehurst Warehouse, the small Texan had concluded that Marshal Benjamin Digbry had carried out his instructions in a most satisfactory manner. There had been no mention of his participation as "*Rapido* Clint." Nor, as his friendly reception at the Binnacle Tavern indicated, had his true identity been exposed. Instead, the peace officer appeared to have been eager to accept full responsibility and take all the credit for the affair. He had let it be believed that "George Breakast" had killed both "Sharpshooter" Schindler and Beguinage, then had been shot by him while resisting arrest. Although the general concensus of opinion among the Tavern's clientele had been surprise that Digbry had achieved such a successful outcome, there was nothing to suggest that his story was not being accepted as the truth.

Remembering his conversation with "Gotz," Dusty had assumed that the anarchist had either been hidden close enough to the warehouse to see what had really happened, or had deduced that "*Rapido* Clint" was involved. He had decided that the former was the more likely to be the correct solution.

Leaving the Tavern when satisfied that there was no more to be learned, the small Texan walked to the area of the dockside at which Crown Prince Rudolph of Bosgravnia and his retinue should have been brought ashore from the steamsloop. The official welcome had not been cancelled and, in addition to the various civic dignitaries who were invited, a good-sized crowd had assembled. His hope that he might come across "Gotz" with other members of the anarchist faction did not materialize. All that he achieved was to witness a demonstration of Governor Stanton Howard's competence as a politician and diplomat.

Using a megaphone to ensure that his words would carry to every member of the crowd, Howard had explained why the Crown Prince was not in the boat which was at that moment coming from the warship. Basically, he had told the truth by stating that the discovery of a plot to assassinate the royal visitor had made the deception necessary. He claimed that it had been implemented so that the local law enforcement officers might have an opportunity to locate and apprehend the would-be murderers. Playing skillfully upon his audience's sense of civic pride, he had removed all the disappointment and resentment that might otherwise have arisen over the measures which had been put into effect. So successful had he been that, by the time he had concluded the explanation, Dusty considered the assembled population were convinced they had been consulted from the beginning and the precautions were being taken with their whole-hearted approval and co-operation.

One aspect of the explanation had been received with

mixed emotions by the small Texan. The announcement that, as a result of Marshal Digbry's investigations and activities, the potential assassins had been located and killed was greeted with applause. Even those members of the community who had previously harboured grave doubts over his abilities as a peace officer, or suspected that his honesty left much to be desired, had joined in the acclaim which he had wrongly been accorded. While Dusty had been pleased by the way in which his own name and participation was concealed, he had also realized that the crowd's response would make the task of bringing about Digbry's removal from office more difficult.

Charlene, *Comtesse de* Petain and Alex von Farlenheim had been part of the Governor's retinue at the dockside, accompanying Howard when he left at the end of the proceedings. So Dusty had not been able to report on the latest developments. Instead, he had set off more in hope than expectancy to try to find where "Breakast" had been residing and to locate "Gotz's" whereabouts. Having failed to do either by nightfall, he had headed for the marshal's office. It was his intention to have Digbry take a message warning the Governor that "*Rapido* Clint" must continue to exist for a few more days. He also wanted to ask if anything had been learned about Beguinage or the dead go-between and request that a watch was kept for the anarchist faction.

Being a prosperous, fast growing and progressive community, Corpus Christie had supplied its municipal law enforcement agency with well-designed accommodation and facilities. The row of stoutly constructed cells at the rear of the building were concealed from the public's view by a dividing wall. At the left side of the large room which faced Dock Street and was allocated for use by the deputies, the marshal had a private office from which to conduct his affairs. To further ensure his privacy, there was no window through which passers by on the street could look in.

The deputies' room was deserted and in darkness when the small Texan arrived. Although the cells at the rear were illuminated, he could hear nothing to suggest they were occupied. Noticing that there was a glow of light under the entrance to the marshal's office, he had crossed towards it. There was no sound from inside, but he had knocked and the door had begun to open. While it had only moved a few inches, he was able to see something of what lay beyond the threshold and, for a moment, the sight froze him in his tracks.

There was, Dusty realized, something unnatural about the rigidly unmoving way in which Digbry was sitting at his desk. He had a ramrod stiffness that was far removed from his normal slouching posture and both hands were pressed on the top of the desk as if he was trying to rise. The expression on his face was an additional indication, if one had been necessary, that all was far from well. Not only were the lips drawn back in a hideous grimace which displayed his tightly clenched teeth, but the wide open eyes were staring glassily and unblinking in the light of the lamp that was suspended from the ceiling.

On the point of advancing to make a closer examination, Dusty noticed there was a trickle of blood which was still not quite congealed running from a small hole at the left side of the marshal's neck on to the collar of his shirt. Instantly, the small Texan appreciated what the sight portended. The peace officer could not have been dead for more than a couple of minutes at the most. So his killer might still be in the office.

Almost without the need for conscious guidance, Dusty's left hand crossed to draw the Colt from the right side holster and his thumb eased the hammer back until it was fully cocked. Then he gave the door a sharp push. The hinges prevented it from opening far enough to strike the wall, but it halted and began to reverse its direction without anything to suggest the killer was lurking behind it. Stepping swiftly across the threshold, with the door swinging until almost closed at his rear, the barrel of his revolver and his gaze made mutual arcs which encompassed every corner of the room.

Although the small Texan had not seen anybody leaving as he was approaching along Dock Street, only he and the corpse were present. However, there was a second door opposite the one through which he had gained admittance to the marshal's office. It offered an exit to the alley alongside the building, removing the need to depart via the main entrance.

Wondering if the killer might still be in the alley, Dusty started to cross the room. Before he had taken more than a couple of steps, his attention was distracted. With a sensation like being touched by an ice-cold hand, he remembered where he had last seen something similar to the marshal's far from pleasant expression. It had been on the face of "Sharpshooter" Schindler, whose throat had been laid open by the blade of Beguinage's knife. However, the wound which had caused the hired killer's death had been much more extensive and serious-looking than Digbry's only visible sign of injury.

Looking along the deserted alley, Dusty did not bother going outside the building. Instead, he closed the door and returned to the desk. Having found himself acting as a peace officer on more than one occasion,[1] he had seen the wisdom of acquiring knowledge of various subjects which would be helpful when investigating crimes. Everything he saw suggested that his education was going to be of service. There was something far out of the ordinary about the manner in which the marshal had met his end. For one thing, all the signs suggested that he must have died very soon after the blow to his throat was struck. Secondly, as far as the small Texan could see, there was no other cause of death.

From medical books he had read, and from what he had been taught while being instructed in the, at that time, little known Japanese martial arts of *ju-jitsu* and *karate*,[2] Dusty was aware there were areas of the human body where death could be caused quickly if pierced by even a comparatively thin, sharp instrument. While he could not remember hearing of such a point in the neck, the carotid artery passed through it carrying blood to the brain. Yet there hardly seemed to have been sufficient loss of blood to have brought an end to Digbry's life, particularly in view of the speed with which it appeared to have happened.

On the point of making a closer examination of the marshal's body to see if there was some other cause of death, Dusty noticed that the top left hand drawer of the desk was open. What he guessed was Digbry's official bunch of keys hung from the lock,

1. New readers can find references to Dusty Fog's career as a peace officer in Footnote 13, Appendix One.—*J.T.E.*
2. New readers, see Paragraph Four, also Footnotes 18, 19 and 20, Appendix One.—*J.T.E.*

but he gave them barely more than a glance. There was only the wallet taken from "Breakast's" body in the drawer. The money it had held was nowhere to be seen. Nor was Beguinage's knife, wrist-sheath and little pot of poison.

A glance told the small Texan that, as was frequently the case with such a piece of furniture, none of the other drawers in the desk was equipped with a lock. He assumed that the marshal had followed the general practice of using the locking drawer as a temporary depository for small items of property instead of unlocking, opening and placing them in the office safe.

So why was there only the *empty* wallet in the drawer?

Thinking of the reluctance Digbry had shown when he was given custody of Beguinage's property, Dusty felt sure that he would not keep it upon his person for any longer than was absolutely necessary. Wanting to get it out of his possession as quickly as possible, he might have taken it when he went to join the other civic dignitaries at the dockside. Then, finding that Dusty was not with the Governor, he could have decided to delay the presentation until they were together at the reception in the evening.

While such devious behaviour would have been consistent with the far from flattering impression Dusty had formed of Digbry, considering it aroused further puzzling speculations. Being eager to demonstrate his "honesty," he would have also taken along the wallet and its contents. Furthermore, having brought back Beguinage's and "Breakast's" property, he would in all probability have kept them together. Appreciating how lethal the knife and poison could be if it should fall into the wrong hands, a more conscientious man might have concluded that they ought to be placed somewhere that offered greater security than the desk locked drawer. However, even if the marshal had shown such forethought, he would have been unlikely to treat the wallet in a different manner to the knife and poison. Nor did there appear to be any reason why he would remove the money if he decided to keep them separately.

Dusty conceded that the marshal's killer could have looted the drawer, but was equally aware of the theory's unanswered questions. Taking the money and leaving the wallet made sense. To be caught while in possession of the latter would be at least suggestive of complicity in the murder. The same applied to carrying off Beguinage's property. Furthermore, while the knife and its sheath might have appeared to be a worthwhile piece of loot, without prior knowledge of its contents, there was nothing to indicate that the pot had any value. Few people other than professional gamblers would have attached any significance to it and even that would be for the wrong reason.

Nor did the theft of such a comparatively small sum of money seem sufficient inducement for the risks entailed in murdering a peace officer in his own office, even if Beguinage's property had also been taken. Which raised the points of why Digbry had opened the drawer and how the killing had been done. The latter was particularly puzzling. The nature of the wound suggested that the means by which it had been inflicted had taken the peace officer unawares. Yet in spite of the small Texan's lack of esteem, he doubted whether Digbry would have given anybody other than a very close acquaintance such an opportunity.

Or a stranger who the marshal might for some reason have considered as being beyond suspicion!

For a man like Digbry, not many people would come into the latter category!

At that point in Dusty's train of thought, a recollection began to stir in his memory.

One of Beguinage's victims in Brownsville was a man whose way of life and current circumstances should have made him even less disposed than Digbry towards accepting strangers at face value. Yet he had paid the penalty of admitting Europe's "premier assassin"—Dusty believed in the guise of a mission padre—to his room.

The face of the dead man in Brownsville had been distorted by an expression almost identical to that of the marshal and "Sharpshooter" Schindler, but there was no wound on his body. He had been killed by drinking poison in a bottle of wine accepted from his visitor. Furthermore, the nature of the wounds which had caused the two latest deaths were vastly different.

And Beguinage had met his end hours before Digbry was murdered!

Looking at the peace officer's only visible wound, Dusty

found himself wishing that he had Doc Leroy with him. While the Wedge cowhand had not yet achieved his ambition to qualify as a doctor of medicine,[3] he had sufficient knowledge to be able to say whether the small puncture in the marshal's throat could cause death as rapidly as it appeared to have done, or if the implement which made it would need to be coated with poison to produce such an effect.

If the latter should be the case, the affair became even more complex and puzzling.

The most logical solution was that, by a coincidence, the killer had arrived armed with a poisonous device. In fact, unlikely as this might appear, Dusty could not think of any other explanation. Certainly Digbry would not have been so stupid, or trusting, to allow *anybody* to apply the poison from Beguinage's receptacle to whatever kind of weapon—even if it appeared to be completely innocuous and harmless—was to be plunged into his throat.

Deciding that he was getting nowhere with his speculations, the small Texan turned his attention to more practical matters. His instincts as a peace officer would not allow him to discard one possibility. In spite of being unable to envisage any reason why the marshal would put Beguinage's property into the safe, while leaving "Breakast's" wallet in the drawer of the desk, he felt it was worth checking if this might be the case. At least, doing so would settle one aspect of the mystery, and he had the means available to satisfy his curiosity.

Removing the bunch of keys from the drawer, Dusty crossed to the safe. Selecting the one which he believed to be appropriate, he found his guess was correct. Having unlocked and opened the door, he looked inside. The contents on the shelves were an untidy jumble, but insufficient in quantity to conceal the European assassin's belongings if they had been buried among any of them.

"God blast, Ike, nobody's bothered to light the lamp!"

"Let's put this son-of-a-bitch in the cells, then I'll do it."

---

3. How Marvin Eldridge "Doc" Leroy—who makes "guest" appearances in various volumes of the Floating Outfit and Waco series—achieved his ambition is told in: DOC LEROY, M.D.—*J.T.E.*

The two comments came to the small Texan's ears, followed by heavy footsteps tramping across the front room. On the point of calling out to whoever had entered, he kept quiet as he realized that to announce his presence under the circumstances might be injudicious. While he could produce a sound motive for his actions, he might not be permitted to make it. Not without creating an undesirable situation. As far as most people in Corpus Christie were concerned, he was a hired killer in search of employment. From all he had heard since his arrival, Digbry's deputies were just as dishonest and corruptible as their superior. However, they were selected for brawn rather than brain. Finding the marshal dead at his desk and "*Rapido* Clint" standing by the open safe, they might draw the most obvious conclusion and be disinclined to listen to his explanation.

Nor was the small Texan enamoured of the prospect of compelling the deputies to let him explain. Not that doing so would be difficult. He had holstered his Colt after looking into the alley, but could draw either it or its mate before bringing the peace officers into the office. Although they would not be likely to resist, having heard of "*Rapido* Clint's" ability with a gun, he would have to exhibit the document which he had shown to Digbry to ensure that he was believed. He felt sure that they would be willing to accept Dusty Fog's explanation, but could not rely upon them to keep the secret of his true identity.

While Dusty would have had misgivings over the course he decided to adopt if he had been dealing with honest and efficient peace officers, he doubted whether the local deputies were competent to investigate their superior's murder. So they would not be hindered in their work if he left them to find Digbry's body in their own time. Waiting until they had escorted their prisoner to the cells, he left by the office's side entrance. Nobody challenged his departure, nor did he hear anything to suggest the peace officers had discovered what had happened to the marshal as he walked along Dock Street in the direction of the hotel.

CHAPTER EIGHT

That Knife Wasn't Aimed at *Me*

"Florence has just been saying that she wonders if you don't like girls, Waco," the beautiful young woman who had been introduced as Lady Winifred Amelia Besgrove-Woodstole remarked, after she had descended from the box of the chuck wagon in which she and the maid had ridden to Corpus Christie. "Or is it English people in general you don't care for?"

Still puzzled by the change which had come over first Mark Counter, then the Ysabel Kid and Waco on being presented to her, the Lady was hoping to discover what had caused it. From the beginning, she had considered that the latter—being the youngest of the trio—might prove to be the most amenable to her persuasive charms and supply the solution. On hearing how the journey to the town was to be made, she had hoped to be granted an opportunity to question him and, having arrived, she felt the time had come.

In addition to having called a halt so that he could ask about the other members of Crown Prince Rudolph's retinue at the livery barn from which the wagon and its team had been hired, Colonel Wilhelm Liebenfrau was making use of the establishment's "back house" to answer the call of nature. His orderly had accompanied him on a similar mission. Waco had stayed with the riding horses, a short distance from the wagon, and was scanning the surrounding buildings. None was closer than fifty yards and all were in darkness, showing no sign of being occupied. From all appearances, the newcomers had the whole area to themselves. It was a situation which offered the Lady the privacy her interrogation required.

"Well now, ma'am," the youngster replied, remembering *not* to remove his hat from his head. He had exchanged his Stetson for the high "sugar-loaf" crowned white Mexican *sombrero* before commencing the return journey from the rendezvous and removing it as he usually would have done when addressing a member of the opposite sex, would have betrayed his disguise. He had also donned and was still wearing a long, voluminous *serape* to conceal almost all of his clothing with the exception of his boots, into which he had tucked the legs of his Levi's pants. "I'm not like one certain jasper I know's I'll leave nameless, called Mark Counter, who spends 'most all of his waking time chasing the gals bow-legged, but I like them just fine I reckon."

"Then it must be that you don't like us English people?" the Lady suggested.

"Can't say's I've met too many of you English folks," Waco answered. "But the Kellers up to the Indian Nations[1] come out to be real nice folks when we got to know them.[2] And they don't come no better nor finer'n lil ole Babsy Smith and her boss-lady up to Mulrooney, Kansas."

"Babsy *Smith*!" the Lady repeated, darting a glance to where her maid was watching and listening on the box of the wagon. Returning her gaze to the young Texan, her voice and face resumed their friendly tone and expression as she continued, "That's an unusual Christian name. Are you sure that she is English?"

"She told me she was a 'Cockney,' or some such, which she allowed's about's English as they come," Waco elaborated, grinning a little at the memory of the buxom and vivacious little blonde saloon-girl with whom he had been on *very* close terms whilst acting as Dusty Fog's least experienced deputy town marshal in Mulrooney.[3] Showing no sign of having noticed the reaction produced by his mention of her, he went on, "And Miss Fre—!" He broke the words off abruptly, realizing that to continue with them might give more away than was desirable and could even supply the information which he suspected

---

1. "Indian Nations": colloquial name for Oklahoma Territory.—*J.T.E.*
2. Waco's meeting with the Keller family is described in: TRIGGER FAST. —*J.T.E.*
3. Told in: THE MAKING OF A LAWMAN and THE TROUBLE BUSTERS.— *J.T.E.*

his interrogator was seeking. "Whooee! Time it's taking the Colonel, he should try drinking some croton oil."

"I don't understand," the Lady declared, genuinely puzzled in spite of the conversation having left the subject in which she was most interested.

"Likely you-all don't have it in England, but it's what folks out here drink when they go out back and can't do what they've gone for," the youngster explained, none too succinctly. "It's always worked pretty well for me, times I've had to use it. Happen you'll excuse such talk in the company of two ladies."

"We will and I think we call something like it 'cascara,'" the Lady replied, a smile twisting at her lips as she understood Waco's meaning. However, appreciating that they were straying from the matter towards which the conversation had previously been directed, she tried to raise it once more. "If your friend really is a Cockney, she must be English. But however did she come to be in the United Sta—?"

"Is there any sign of His Highness yet, young man?" Colonel Liebenfrau called, striding as smartly as if marching on a parade from the well lit interior of the livery barn with his orderly following and carrying a lantern. They were both wearing clothing of range country style and, although it no longer carried the sabre on its slings, the officer still retained his military belt with its holstered revolver. However, as many men who had served in the Confederate or Union Armies made use of similar equipment, this was not detrimental to the disguise. "Neither he nor the other party have been here yet."

"Can't see anything of them, Colonel," Waco answered, without commenting that the darkness and the various buildings around the barn rendered any sighting at a distance most unlikely. He was not sorry to have had the discussion with the Lady brought to an end, so pointed out, "We came in along the Coast Road, which's a shorter way of hitting town than either Lon or Mark'll be coming. But they shouldn't be too much longer afore they show up. Happen you're so minded, we can wait for them here instead of going straight to the Blaby place."

"I would like to go straight there, Colonel, so that I can

change into something a trifle more suitable for the reception," the Lady suggested. "But if you would rather stay here until His Highness arrives, perhaps Waco could take me there."

"Mark said's I was to take you-all to the Blaby place, Colonel," the youngster pointed out, before the Personal Attendant could reply and, while polite, his voice held a tone which brooked no argument. His eyes flickered to the Lady and he finished, "So, much's I'd admire to go along with you, ma'am, that's what I have to do. Either we all go, or we all stay put until the others come."

Having heard the instructions to which Waco was referring, Liebenfrau gave a stiff nod of agreement. In spite of his apprehensions over the current situation, he admired the youngster for being willing to carry out orders which might be contrary to the wishes of a person of superior social standing.

The Personal Attendant might have the appearance of being a typical Prussian-trained senior officer, but he possessed a flexibility of thought and a willingness to accept unconventional tactics or methods which was not a general character trait of men educated under that exacting military code. While he had had the misgivings over one aspect, he was willing to concede that the arrangements to ensure the safe arrival of Crown Prince Rudolph in Corpus Christie had been planned with considerable forethought. Nor could he fault the way in which they were being carried out.

Not only had attire suitable for their surroundings been provided for the royal visitor and his retinue, but there was sufficient of it in various sizes to ensure each member found garments to fit him. Nor had the disguising ended there. The men who were to act as escort had helped the deception by making alterations to their own appearances. What was more, although they had set out that morning for the rendezvous riding their usual mounts, they had had other less distinctive and eye-catching horses waiting about two miles from the town upon which they could make the return journey. Even having the visitors bring some of their baggage ashore had been a furtherance of the scheme. When the matter was "accidentally" mentioned by the captain and selected members of the U.S.S. *Nantucket*'s crew, it was hoped that any would-be assassins who heard would assume their intended victim was to be kept away from Corpus Christie until at least the following day.

However, a further precaution had disturbed Liebenfrau when he was told of it. In spite of appreciating how splitting up the party into three groups and travelling by different routes would lessen the chance of the ploy being detected, he had objected on learning that he and the Crown Prince would not be continuing the journey together. He had pointed out that, in his capacity as Personal Attendant, he should accompany his sovereign lord at all times. Once again, it had fallen upon Rudolph to insist upon accepting Mark Counter's wishes. So Liebenfrau had ridden along the Coast Road at the side of the chuck wagon, which was driven by his orderly. The Lady and her maid were passengers and Waco had acted as their guide.

Apart from Liebenfrau using a shotgun to bring down a few quail, the journey had been uneventful. A very careful watch was kept, but the party had neither met nor seen any other human beings. Carrying out his instructions, the youngster had made sure that they did not come into sight of Corpus Christie during the hours of daylight. It had been dark for almost an hour when they arrived at what proved to be a deserted livery barn.

While the Personal Attendant had not mentioned his misgivings, it had been apparent to the others of his party that he was uneasy. They had realized that he was having difficulty in reconciling himself to being separated from the Crown Prince when there was a possibility of danger.

"We will go to the mansion, Lady Winifred," Liebenfrau declared, stopping and looking over his shoulder at the orderly, reverting to his native tongue. *"Bleiben sie hie—!"*

Something that glittered metallically hissed from the darkness. Travelling at high speed, it almost touched the Colonel's neck in passing. In fact, if he had not paused with the intention of telling his orderly to stay at the livery barn until the arrival of the Crown Prince, the missile would have struck him. Missing, it sank into the side of the wagon and, vibrating, revealed itself to be a knife.

Swinging around, trying to decide from whence the

weapon had come, Waco sent his hands flashing downwards. He was acting with the trained reflexes of a highly competent gun-fighter, but for once found them to be putting him at a disadvantage. Instead of enfolding the staghorn butts of his Army Colts, he found himself grasping the harsh material of the blanket-like *serape*.

Letting out a startled oath in guttural German, the orderly showed presence of mind by throwing aside the lantern. Its light was extinguished as it struck the ground, bringing darkness to the side of the wagon upon which the party were standing and rendering them far less open targets for the unseen assailant. Having done so, grabbing at the holster on the right side of his belt, he started to run in the general direction from which the knife had come.

Employing language which he would not have thought of using in the presence of two women under less trying circumstances, Waco sent the *sombrero* flying as he dragged the offending *serape* over his head. Although as yet he had not grasped the full significance of what he had seen, the way in which the knife had been thrown and dug into the side of the wagon warned him against taking chances when going up against its owner. So he had no intention of advancing until he had rid himself of what might prove an impediment to rapid movement.

"Look after the ladies, Colonel!" the youngster snapped, tossing the garment aside and noticing that the beautiful blonde was producing a Remington Double Derringer from the right side pocket of her jacket.

Drawing his Colts, without waiting to see whether Liebenfrau was obeying, Waco moved forward. He had not seen exactly where the knife had been thrown from, so did not follow the orderly. Instead, he made for the opposite end of the nearest building. Before he had covered half the distance, certain factors began to imprint themselves upon his mind. However, he did not allow them to distract him or to interfere with his cautious scrutiny of the terrain ahead.

The youngster's range of vision was extremely restricted. None of the light from the doors of the barn spread even as far as his present position. Because of other buildings beyond that which he was approaching, he could not see if the alley had an occupant. So he slowed his pace, moving warily and employing all the knowledge of night fighting he had accrued from that acknowledged master, the Ysabel Kid.

Showing less restraint and caution, the Bosgravnian orderly was already entering the alley at the other end of the building. He had succeeded in drawing his revolver, but Waco considered that his behaviour was ill-advised, even reckless in the extreme. Watching the man disappear, the youngster strained his ears to catch the slightest warning that the soldier might be paying for the rashness, and to try and detect any lurking enemy in the blackness towards which he himself was heading.

Flattening his back against the front wall of the building, Waco glanced at the wagon. He found that Liebenfrau had acted upon his instructions. From what he could make out, the Personal Attendant and the Lady had gone around the vehicle and the maid was no longer on its box. Satisfied that they were sheltered, at least until whoever had thrown the knife moved to another position, he gave his attention to the work in hand.

Carefully, pleased that he had already discarded the *sombrero*, the youngster crouched and peered around the corner. Even from the lower position he was unable to see anything in the inky darkness of the alley, and he was painfully aware that, on entering, he could be sky-lined for whoever was further along.

"Oh hell!" Waco mused, as he started to ease himself around the corner. "Who wants to live forever, 'cepting maybe m—!"

The thought was terminated as the youngster heard a slight scuffle from the other side and rear of the building. It was followed by an exclamation he could not understand, but knew was being made by the Bosgravnian orderly. The words ended in a hissing gasp of pain which was followed by light footsteps departing rapidly.

Swinging around, Waco raced by the front of the building. He showed no hesitation over turning the corner on reaching the other end. However, he slowed his pace and continued his advance with the care he had previously exhibited once he was in the alley. While there had been the suggestion that somebody was leaving the vicinity hurriedly, it was not necessarily the knife-thrower. With that disturbing thought in mind, stepping warily so each foot felt ahead to make sure it did not strike anything which would make a sound and betray him, he went onwards. There were the usual night noises of a busy town in the background to drown his furtive movements, but they would also muffle any made by a person waiting in ambush.

Nothing happened as the youngster continued his advance. Reaching the rear of the building, he adopted the same precautions as he had at the front. The visibility was a trifle better, but he found neither pleasure nor relief in what he saw. A few feet away, a bulky dark shape was huddled half sitting, half lying against the end of the next structure. He did not need to exercise his deductive prowess to know what it was.

After scanning the surrounding area without detecting any sign of human life, Waco holstered his left hand Colt and walked forward. Kneeling he reached and touched the unmoving body of the orderly. He remembered a technique he had learned from Doc Leroy and started to feel under the man's chin. Something wet met his questing fingers, but he was unable to locate the pulsing movement which would be a sign of life. Yet there did not appear to be much blood flowing, nor any extensive injury to account for it if that was what the warm and slightly sticky liquid was.

Having satisfied himself that the orderly was dead, the youngster gazed around. He accepted the futility of trying to find whoever had struck the soldier down. So he swung around and his toe kicked something. Wondering if it might be the murder weapon, he bent and felt until he found and picked it up. It appeared to be a fairly thin piece of almost round wood with a bone hook at one end. Puzzled, he took it with him as he started to retrace his footsteps through the alley. As he went, he dropped the other Colt back into leather.

"Where is Hoffmeyer?" Liebenfrau demanded, emerging from behind the wagon as the young Texan approached.

"Dead," Waco replied, picking up the lantern.

"*Dead?*" the Personal Attendant demanded and his voice showed concern. "How?"

"I don't know, Colonel," Waco admitted, hooking the stick he had found on to his gunbelt and reaching into his Levi's hip pocket. "That's why I've come back for the lantern, so I can find out."

"I'll come with you!" Liebenfrau stated.

"Might be best if you didn't, Colonel," the youngster said gently. "Whoever killed him might still be around and that knife wasn't aimed at *me.*"

"I don't understand," Liebenfrau declared, pausing instead of setting off as had been his intention.

"If they'd wanted me, I was stood there and giving them a clear throw for a spell afore you come out of the barn," the youngster explained. "Which makes it look to me like this toad-sticker was thrown at *you.* Only I'm damned if I can make out *how.*"

While the conversation was taking place, Waco had extracted and rasped a match on the seat of his pants. In spite of its rough handling, the lantern responded when he applied the flame to the wick and he went to examine the knife. Its blade was an unusual shape, at least ten inches in length and resembling a butcher's sharpening steel rather than a conventional weapon. As he was delivering his next to last pronouncement, he grasped the guardless hilt and needed to apply considerable strength before he was able to draw the point from the side of the wagon.

"What do you mean, *how?*" Liebenfrau barked.

"It's fifty yards at least to where the jasper who threw it was standing," the youngster elaborated. "I'd say that not even Lon could send his bowie knife that far and have it sink in as deep as this toad-sticker did."

"What is that you have in your belt, Waco," the Lady inquired, she and her maid having followed the Bosgravnian.

"I don't know," the youngster replied. "It was lying close by your man, Colonel. At first I thought it might have been what killed him, but if it was, I don't know how it was used either."

"May I see it?" the Lady requested and, receiving a confirmatory nod, lifted the device from the gunbelt. Turning it in her hands, she studied it with particular attention to the almost flattened wood on the side of the bone hook. "It looks like the end of a walking-stick, or more likely an umbrella. Can I have the knife, please?"

"Why sure," Waco assented, although Liebenfrau was moving restless and clearly wanted to go to the dead orderly. Glancing at the spike-like blade, he moved it closer to the lantern and went on, "Hey though. Could be this thing's been used not too long back. There's what looks like dried blood on the point."

"Be careful!" the Lady ejaculated. "That could be poison, not blood!"

On the point of demanding that Waco accompany him to the scene of the murder, the Personal Attendant refrained. Even before they had set sail from Europe, he had found the young Englishwoman to be remarkably intelligent and knowledgeable on more than one subject which was not normally regarded as being the province of her sex. During the voyage, he had seen further sufficient examples of her acumen to consider that whatever she might have to say could prove interesting. Certainly she had not made her request to examine the piece of wood out of idle curiosity. So he was willing to wait until he heard what she had to say before taking his departure.

Taking the knife by its blade gingerly, the Lady rested it on the flattened side of the stick and slipped the end of the hilt under the curve of the bone hook. Holding the weapon in position, she raised the device above her right shoulder.

"What does that tell you, ma'am?" Waco inquired, as the blonde lowered her hand.

"I'm only hazarding a guess, of course," the Lady replied, holding forward the device with the weapon still in position. "But this could be the means by which the knife was thrown so far and with such force. It reminds me of a *woomera* I saw in the British Museum."

"A what?" the youngster asked and heard Liebenfrau give a low hiss.

"It's a device that the Australian aborigines—natives—use

to help when throwing a spear,"[4] the Lady elaborated, noticing how the Personal Attendant was nodding in understanding and agreement. "According to a friend who has been Down Under and seen one in use, it will send a seven-foot-long-spear for about a hundred and fifty yards and can kill a man at more than half of that distance."

"Whee-doggie!" Waco ejaculated. "I've never seen nor heard of any such thing, but I'm not saying it couldn't be. I don't reckon that anybody could throw a knife this far without something to help it along. And, happen that is poison on the point, you wouldn't need to sink it in deep to kill. Just a nick could do that, happen the poison's strong enough."

"Come!" Liebenfrau barked, deciding that there had been enough discussion and wanting to go to his orderly.

"I reckon it'd be better if you stayed here while I go and scout around a mite, Colonel," Waco suggested. "Whoever killed your man could be waiting out there to have a second chance at you-all."

"I'm not afraid!" Liebenfrau growled.

"Being afraid don't come into it," the youngster stated. "Seems like good sense not to take chances unless you have to."

"My mind is made up," the Personal Attendant declared. "Two pairs of eyes are better than one, it doubles the chance of seeing something."

"I'm not gainsaying it," Waco drawled, knowing he could not change the older man's mind. "All right, let's go. Do me a lil favour, though."

"What is it?" Liebenfrau asked.

---

4. Forming an extension to the thrower's arm and, as its front end moves faster than the hand holding it, the *woomera* helps to generate a centrifugal force that greatly increases the velocity when the spear leaves it at the highest point of its arc. Held above and behind the shoulder with the hook upwards and the spear pointing forward, it is operated by a swing of the arm and snap of the wrist. While the *woomera* is now primarily associated with the Australian aboriginies, a similar device was used by prehistoric *Cro-Magnon* men and various primitive people prior to the discovery of how to make and employ a bow and arrows.—*J.T.E.*

"Stay out of the light," the youngster requested. "I don't want to have to face Mark and Lon, much less Dusty, should you-all get killed."

"I will do as you ask," the Personal Attendant promised, after giving a snort which the Lady suspected was registering a mixture of surprise and amusement at the reason offered by the Texan for the concern over his well-being. "Now come!"

"Take these and wait for us in the barn, Florence," the blonde instructed, holding out the objects which she had been examining.

"That shotgun the Colonel was using on the birds while we were cming here is in the wagon," the maid replied, showing no apprehension over being left behind or taking the knife and throwing device. "So I'll do the waiting in there, if that's all right with you, Miss Amel—Lady Winifred, I mean!"

"Do as you wish," the Lady authorized, after glancing to find out whether the two men had heard what was being said and deciding, as they continued to walk away without looking around, that they had not. There was a faintly chiding note in her voice, discernible to one who knew her as well as the maid, when she went on, "But, considering that there's already something puzzling those young men about me and how intelligent they've shown themselves to be, don't make a mistake like *that* again."

CHAPTER NINE

He Might Not Be Dead

"A gentleman asked me to give you this, sir," the desk clerk of the Portside Hotel told Dusty Fog, holding out a sealed envelope as well as the room key he had come to collect.

"Would it be anybody I know?" the small Texan inquired, accepting both items.

"I haven't seen him before," the clerk answered. "But he looked like an officer from the merchant ship of some kind."

"Thickset *hombre* between your height and mine, with a beard?" Dusty suggested and, receiving a nod of confirmation, went on, "Sounds like it was good old Mr. Gotz."

"He didn't say his name," the clerk stated, sounding aggrieved by the omission.

"Must have been him then," Dusty declared, unable to resist the temptation to tease the well-padded and pompous man on the other side of the desk. "He's sort of shy and retiring. *Gracias* anyways. I've been waiting for this."

"Very good—sir," the clerk replied, with ill-concealed disapproval and turned away.

"Damn it if I'm not starting to act like Waco," the small Texan mused, tearing open the flap of the envelope and walking from the desk. "I'm going to have to change such blasted ways."

Ascending the stairs to the first floor, Dusty extracted and read the sheet of paper from the envelope. He found that he was invited to call at an address in the waterfront district to discuss his terms at eleven o'clock that night.

In spite of a sense of satisfaction over the way in which the anarchist faction had responded to his bait, Dusty did not allow it to command his entire attention. He was aware that constant alertness was a vital necessity when engaged upon the kind of mission which had brought him to Corpus Christie.

Nor did knowing that he had killed Beguinage make him think he could relax his vigilance. Even if it had, one of his precautions had been put into effect before he set out for the Edgehurst Warehouse.

Every time Dusty had left his room at the hotel, he had employed a ruse learned from the Rebel Spy by fastening a piece of black thread from the top of the door to its jamb. Nobody could enter without breaking it, but it would not offer sufficient resistance for its presence to be detected.

Glancing upwards instinctively as he was tucking the letter into his pants' right hip pocket, the small Texan found that the thread had been snapped. He knew what the sight portended. Somebody had entered his room since he had taken his departure. Whoever it was had had no right to be there. Since one of their number had nearly fallen a victim to Beguinage's snake-in-a-box trap, the hotel's maids always made a habit of arriving to perform their duties while Dusty was present. He had been only too pleased that it should be so. In fact, he had handed out gratuities to ensure that they were finished and did not need to return when he was absent.

All of which suggested there had been, or still was, an intruder in the room!

Walking by the door, Dusty halted at the left instead of in front of it. Standing with his back to the wall, he listened for a moment without hearing anything to suggest that his unauthorized visitor was still in the room. He was disinclined to accept that whoever had entered was no longer there, and therefore he decided what action he would take. Before putting his plan into operation, he glanced in each direction to make sure that he had the passage to himself.

If anybody had been near by, they would have witnessed an exhibition of the ambidextrous prowess Dusty had developed during his early years. In part, it had been a means to distract attention from his small size and it had continued to serve him well all through his life. Simultaneously, with his left hand reaching around to insert the key into the lock, the right crossed to slip the Colt from the near-side holster. Then he timed the cocking of the hammer with the turning of the key so that the two sets of clicking sounded together.

Having unlocked the door, Dusty twisted at its knob and

shoved hard. With its hinges creaking slightly, it began to swing open. He went across the threshold in a fast dive and found that taking the precaution with the piece of thread had been worthwhile. However, in spite of its warning, he was anything but out of danger.

The room was occupied!

But there were two intruders, not one!

Opposite the door, an armed man was sitting on the sill of the open window. He held a sawed-off shotgun with its twin barrels aligned at what would have been chest height on a person of average size who was entering the room. Also clad in worn range clothes, the second intruder was to the right. Apparently he had been examining the contents of the wardrobe, but had started to turn on hearing that somebody was entering.

For all the man at the window's position of readiness, he appeared to be surprised to see who was coming in. Instead of trying to correct his point of aim immediately, he stared at the small Texan and his face began to register amazement. Right hand dipping towards the butt of a holstered Army Colt, his companion duplicated his reaction.

Such hesitation was fatal when dealing with a gun-fighter of Dusty Fog's calibre.

Landing on the floor, the small Texan was already slanting his weapon in the direction of the more immediately dangerous intruder. Nor had he the slightest doubt over how he must deal with the situation. Sighting as he alighted, he squeezed off a shot. The .45 bullet flew to its intended mark and took the man with the shotgun between the eyes. As an aid to escape in the event of a fire, the two sections of the hotel's upstairs windows opened outwards instead of sliding up or down. So there was nothing to prevent him from being tumbled backwards under the impact. Taking his weapon with him as he fell, it went off to send its charge of buckshot harmlessly into the night sky.

Even as the shotgun was bellowing outside the room, Dusty was preparing to defend himself against his second adversary. Rolling on to his left side, he swung the Colt in the appropriate direction. Despite the suggestion that the man had been taken aback, either by the sight of him or by the way in which he had entered the room, he knew there would be no time to make even a rapid aim. Already the other was throwing off his shock sufficiently to have resumed bringing the revolver from its holster.

So, instead of trying to align the sights, Dusty kept the barrel of the Colt moving. While his right forefinger held the trigger depressed, he used the heel of his left hand to pull on the spur of the hammer and operate the single action mechanism. Five times in less than three seconds he repeated the motion, directing the bullets that were being propelled from the muzzle along slightly different routes. Three missed, but by an ever decreasing margin. Nor were they entirely wasted, for they produced the effect he had hoped they might.

Seeing the flame and smoke erupting from the Colt held by a man he believed to be a deadly efficient professional killer, the second assailant fumbled his draw. He was not given another opportunity to recover his wits. The fourth and fifth bullets entered his chest about three inches apart. Letting his own weapon slip from his grasp, he reeled and sprawled to the floor.

Rising swiftly, Dusty drew and cocked his second Colt while returning the empty revolver to its holster. As he walked forward, keeping the weakly moving man under observation and ready to take any further action that might prove necessary, he found himself pondering on what had just happened.

On discovering that somebody had entered his room and realizing that whoever it was could still be there, Dusty had expected it was almost certainly someone who had the intention of trying to kill him. When he had first seen the men, he had been sure that his summation was correct. They had been pointed out to him at the Binnacle tavern as low-quality hard cases and frequent companions of the trio hired—by Beguinage he suspected, although he was unable to obtain evidence to support the assumption—to ambush him on the street one night. However, considering the way in which the men had behaved on seeing him, he was starting to wonder if he had drawn the wrong conclusion.

There had been nothing to suggest either of the pair was involved in the abortive ambush. Nor did what little the small Texan had seen and heard of them lead him to believe they were the kind who would seek him out with the intention of avenging the two men he had been compelled to kill. In his opinion, they would require a much stronger motive than revenge before they tangled with "*Rapido* Clint."

While the pair would not have any scruples where committing crimes was concerned, Dusty doubted whether they had entered his room merely to rob it. For one thing, wearing such cheap and shoddy clothing would make gaining admittance to the upper floors of a place like the Portside Hotel almost impossible. Of course, they could have had an accomplice on the premises to let them in, and the selection of his room might have been no more than a coincidence. That would explain why they were so surprised when they saw who was bursting in on them.

Voices and footsteps approaching rapidly along the passage diverted Dusty from his train of thought, but he did not turn to find out who was coming. The wounded man was staring up at him with pain-glazed eyes and he knew that the end was near. Kicking the revolver aside, he holstered his Colt and bent forward.

"Why'd you come here?" Dusty inquired quietly.

"Sh-Sh—" the man gasped. "She s-said thi-this—her hus-husband's room."

"Who did?" the small Texan asked, still gently yet urgently.

A convulsive shudder racked the man and blood burst from his mouth. Then his head hinged forward and his body went limp. Dusty straightened up, knowing there would be no reply to his question.

"Wh-What happened?" asked a familiar voice, trying to make the words sound like a demand for information rather than a quavering request.

Looking over his shoulder, Dusty saw the desk clerk entering with two well-dressed men close behind. They were staring from him to the lifeless intruder, and they came to a halt as he turned towards them.

"I found this hombre and another here when I came in," Dusty answered, truthfully if not expansively.

"*Another*!" the clerk yelped, taking a step backwards and

looking around with an even greater display of alarm. "Wh-Where is he?"

"You'll find him lying outside," the small Texan explained. "He fell out of the window when I shot him."

"You shot him too?" the clerk almost gobbled.

"It seemed like a reasonable thing to do," Dusty replied. "Seeing that he was pointing a sawed-off scattergun at me."

"Why were they waiting for you?" the taller of the well-dressed men put in, stepping by the clerk.

"One thing's for sure," Dusty drawled, continuing to act as *"Rapido* Clint" might under similar circumstances. "It wasn't because I'd asked them up to take coffee with me." Then swinging his gaze to the hotel's employee, his voice took on a rasp of exasperation. "God damn it all, what kind of place is this? I near on got killed by a son-of-a-bitching copperhead somebody'd left in my room just after I got here. And now *this*."

"I—I assure you that nothing like it has ever happened here before," the clerk protested, loyalty to the hotel overriding the alarm he was experiencing over being the object of what he assumed to be indignation from a man rumour claimed was a notorious professional gun-fighter. "We are a most respect—"

"It looks like you're a man who's got more than his fair share of enemies, Mr.—Stormont," the taller of the residents commented, stepping forward.

"Meaning?" Dusty asked and, in keeping with the character he was playing, his attitude had taken on more than a hint of a challenge.

"From what I've heard," the man replied, showing no sign of being perturbed by the threatening tone and posture. "This isn't the first time you've killed men in Corpus Christie."

The small Texan knew his interrogator to be the owner of a small, but prosperous shipping line. By all accounts, his reputation for honesty and courage had been earned the hard way and was well deserved. So he was unlikely to let himself be frightened or browbeaten, even by somebody he might have heard was dangerous to cross. However, Dusty had no intention of telling any more than was absolutely necessary, and thought that he might be able to avoid the need to do so.

"Those two that night on the street were figuring to rob

me," the small Texan countered. "At least, that's what the marshal told me after he'd been asking around town about them."

"That's true," the clerk supplemented, as the shipowner gave a sniff that was redolent of anything but respect for the peace officer's judgement. The clerk, hoping to act as a peacemaker and avert any further disturbance on the premises, continued. "And he said that the snake must have been left by somebody who was trying to kill the man who had the room before Mr. Stormont."

"That's the way the marshal figured it out," Dusty went on, pleased with the interruption and continuing to press home what he hoped would be an advantage. "Which, from what that *hombre* by the wall told me just afore he died, it could be right."

"What did he say?" the shipowner asked.

"Something about them being sent to this room by a woman so's they could gun down her husband," Dusty replied. "And, mister, *I'm* not married, nor ever have been."

"Then they couldn't have been after you!" the clerk stated, throwing an imploring look at the shipowner and hoping his declaration would be accepted.

"They couldn't," Dusty agreed, but he was wondering what the truth of the matter might be in spite of his apparent sincerity.

"Where are you going, Lady Winifred?" Colonel Wilhelm Liebenfrau asked, glancing behind him as he and Waco walked away from the livery barn.

"With you," the beautiful young woman replied and, although she did not continue with, "of course," the words were implied by her demeanour.

"That is out of the question!" the Personal Attendant declared, exuding an equal determination and halting to turn with military precision. "Whoever killed Hoffmeyer—!"

"He might not be dead," the Lady interrupted.

"Was ist das?" Liebenfrau almost bellowed, so startled by the suggestion that he made the inquiry, "What is this?" in his native German and swung a furiously accusing gaze at the tall blond youngster.

"There is a slender chance he might be alive," the Lady asserted, before the Texan—who was also facing her—could think of a comment. Raising her right hand in a placatory gesture, she went on, "No offence, Waco, but you aren't a qualified doctor. Nor, from what you told us, were you able to make a close examination in the darkness."

"That's for sure," the youngster admitted, sounding worried. "But he looked and even felt dead 'cepting that I couldn't find much of a wound to show how it was done."

"There are some kinds of poison which induce such a deep stupor that it can be mistaken for death," the Lady explained. "If one of them was used, I might be able to help Hoffmeyer. So let's not waste any more time talking, the delay could prove fatal."

"It's worth a chance, Colonel," Waco stated, swinging on his heel. As he and the Bosgravnian set off with the Englishwoman between them, he continued, "Anyway, it's not likely whoever put him down'll chance coming back. Not real close, at least and, even if he's got more of them fancy knives, he's lost the doohickey that he threw the other with. Hey though, where is it?"

"I left it and the knife with my maid," the Lady replied.

"Is that wise?" Liebenfrau asked. "To leave her alone, I mean. There is nobody at the barn."

"Don't worry about Florence," the Lady answered, with complete confidence. "She's going to stay in the wagon. Your shotgun is there and she knows how to use it. So she can take care of herself."

"*Bueno*," Waco drawled, wondering if all English maids had a similar competence. "Will you-all take the lantern, Colonel, and I'll go ahead, to scout around and make sure that *hombre* hasn't come back."

"Very well," the Personal Attendant consented stiffly.

Relieved of what would have been a dangerous encumbrance, the youngster went forward at a faster pace. On reaching the place where the orderly had fallen, although sure that he had been correct in his diagnosis, he could not resist the urge to repeat the test. It came almost as a relief to feel the flesh was colder than on the previous occasion and once more to be unable to detect the throbbing of the vein in the neck.

Straightening up, he carried out the task for which he had left his companions. When satisfied that there was no danger, he returned to the corpse and called Liebenfrau's name.

Even though Waco had been convinced that life was extinct when he had conducted his first examination, what he saw in the light thrown by the lantern gave him a shock. It also provided indisputable evidence that Hoffmeyer had indeed been dead and not merely in a deep stupor. While there was only a small hole in the left side of his throat, from which a minute trickle of blood had run, his face was contorted by an expression of unspeakable agony.

"Gott in himmel!" Liebenfrau gasped.

"Son-of-a-bitch!" Waco growled. "I've seen a fair slew of dead men, but never one who looked like *that*!"

"I have!" the Lady said, in barely more than a whisper. "The wound and facial expression are identical to those of an uncle of mine who was murdered by that assassin you told us has been hired to kill Prince Rudolph."

"Beguinage?" the Personal Attendant spat out and seemed on the point of saying something more, but did not.

"If it was him that tried to put you down, you was lucky, Colonel," Waco drawled. "What I've heard, 'cepting for Dusty, everybody else he gone after's wound up dead."

CHAPTER TEN

Doesn't He *Ever* Shoot Anybody

"Hot damn, Dusty!" Waco burst out, oblivious of the distinguished company who were listening, as the small Texan concluded a description of his side of the day's events. "What in hell's going on? From what you say, whoever made wolf bait[1] of poor old Hoffmeyer must be the one's put the marshal under."

Events had moved rapidly since Dusty had surprised the two men in his room. The desk clerk had been ready and willing to accept that Dusty Fog's mistaken identity, or at least wrong information about him, had caused the shooting at the Portside Hotel; but the shipowner had been less obliging. However, in view of the next development, he had seen the difficulty facing him if he should attempt to press the issue further.

Being experienced in his duties despite his pomposity, the clerk had not wasted time when he had heard the disturbance upstairs. Before coming up to investigate, he had sent the bell boy to summon the town marshal. Returning alone, the youngster brought the news that Digbry had been murdered and said all the deputies claimed they were too busy to come to the hotel.

Sharing Dusty's unexpressed sentiments with regard to the municipal peace officers' incompetence and venality, the shipowner had not considered their absence would be of any great loss. He had also been surprised by the small Texan's suggestion that, as the local authorities were unavailable, the two of

---

1. "Made wolf bait": to kill. Derived from the practice of shooting an animal and, having poisoned the carcass, leaving it where it fell to be eaten by wolves.—*J.T.E.*

them should go the the Blaby mansion and put the matter in the hands of Governor Stanton Howard's staff. Realizing that he was not sufficiently skillful with a gun to impose his will upon a man he had heard was a very proficient *pistolero valiente*, he had seen no objections to agreeing.

Once they were in the privacy of the shipowner's carriage, Dusty had disclosed his true identity. Telling him something of his assignment, he had requested and been granted cooperation. On reaching their destination and finding that other guests were already beginning to assemble, he contrived, with the shipowner's assistance, to reach the owner of the mansion's ground floor study unnoticed. At the Governor's request, he had waited until the royal visitor's retinue arrived before telling his story.

Almost two hours had gone by before the meeting could commence. It was comprised of the Ysabel Kid, Waco, Howard, Colonel Wilhelm Liebenfrau, the sheriff of Neuces County—of which Corpus Christie was the seat, although he had not yet taken up his duties—and, out of courtesy, the shipowner. Their host, Senator Cornelius Blaby, Crown Prince Rudolph of Bosgravnia, Major the Baron von Goeringwald, Captain Fritz von Farlenheim and Mark Counter were not present, it having been considered that their absence from the reception could arouse unwanted attention.

"It looks that way," Dusty admitted to Waco, seeing that most of the party appeared to be in agreement with the blond youngster's comment. "Or it's one hell of a coincidence."

"Too much of one for my liking," the Ysabel Kid declared and, once again, there was general concurrence. "Anyways, likely the Colonel can tell us something about Beguinage."

"What do you mean?" Liebenfrau growled, swinging a glowering gaze at the black dressed Texan.

"Going by what the Prince told me on the way into town, you're the head he-hooper of his police force," the Kid explained, puzzled by the vehemence of the question. "So I figured's you'd find out all you could about any hired killer's might get paid to take his scalp."

"I try to," the Personal Attendant conceded, his voice retaining its brusque timbre although his ramrod-straight posture relaxed a trifle.

"Then you'd maybe know what kind of sneaky meanness he uses to do his killing," the Kid went on. "He put a copperhead into the soft-shell's[2] room in Brownsville, same's he tried here on Dusty, and he used poisoned wine to put down Dink Sproxton. Then there was the knife he used to give "Sharpshooter" Schindler another mouth *under* the chin and figured on doing the same to Dusty with. That was poisoned as well. Doesn't he *ever* shoot anybody like a good red-blooded American hired gun?"

"I've never heard of him doing so," Liebenfrau stated. "From all the reports I've seen, he prefers more subtle methods."

"The Lady allows he made wolf bait of her uncle in the same way that Hoffmeyer and the marshal were killed," Waco remarked. "Which, happen it isn't subtle'll do for me until something comes along that is."

"There's just one thing about that, though," the sheriff pointed out. "Captain Fog had killed Beguinage hours before either of them died."

Tall, well made and in his early forties, Elvis Tragg belonged to a family who were prominent in Texas law enforcement.[3] He had only recently been appointed sheriff of Neuces County, but had gained a reputation for scrupulous honesty and efficiency elsewhere. Although he had not yet made a start, he had known that his primary task would be to purge the corruption that was rife in the Corpus Christie town marshal's department. The opportunity to investigate Digbry's death would make it easier for him to obtain evidence against the no less venal deputies. However, being conscientious, he could not overlook the serious set of events he had heard mentioned in the study.

"He only asks the fool questions," the Kid drawled, throwing a mock derisive look at the blond youngster. "Then he sits

2. "Soft shell": derogatory name for a radical liberal intellectual.—*J.T.E.*
3. And still are. See the author's Rockabye County series covering the duties of a modern Texas sheriff, Jack Tragg, and his deputies.—*J.T.E.*

back and lets the folks with brains come up with the smart answers."

"Which let's *you-all* out of ever giving 'em, you blasted slit-eyed quarter *Pehnane*[4] war-whoop," Waco countered, directing an equally well simulated disdainful glare at his Indian-dark *amigo*. Then he became more serious as, swinging his gaze to the leader of the floating outfit, he went on, "Could it've been Beguinage who sent those three yahoos's tried to bushwhack you that night, Dusty?"

"I've been thinking some on those lines myself," the small Texan admitted. "And I haven't been able to come up with anybody else who could have. It wasn't somebody with an old grudge against "*Rapido* Clint," because he didn't exist until I got here and he didn't make any other enemies in town."

"Might it've been somebody who recognized *you* and figured it gave a good chance to get evens?" Tragg suggested.

"That's possible, although I don't recall seeing anybody who I'd had a run in with somewhere else," Dusty conceded. "Word has it that they'd got friendly with a foreign girl in a saloon they used on the night they came after me. She'd only started there that afternoon, left with them and never went back. Did you ever hear of Beguinage having a woman for a partner, Colonel?"

"No," the Personal Attendant answered. "Why?"

"If he did, it could explain some of the things that haven't been setting right with me," Dusty replied, wondering if he wasn't imagining that there was something almost defensive in the Bosgravnian's attitude each time he was called upon to supply information about the assassin. "Like who would Digbry have let come close enough to kill him the way it must have happened."

"Hell, yes!" Waco ejaculated. "It'd have to be somebody he knowed real well, or figured wouldn't—or couldn't—do him any harm."

"Are you-all saying that a *woman* could've killed Digbry the way it was done?" Tragg protested. In spite of his general

4. New readers, see Appendix Three for explanation of the word, "*Pehnane*".—*J.T.E.*

competence as a peace officer he had something of what would come to be referred to as a "male chauvinist pig" attitude where members of the "weaker" sex were concerned.

"There haven't been many owlhoots who could touch the Bad Bunch when it come to out-and-out ornery meanness, sheriff," the blond youngster answered, mentioning a band of vicious and murderous female criminals who had nearly killed Dusty and Mark before their activities were brought to an end.[5] "And, by all accounts, Bat Gooch was a better'n fair bounty hunter. But he got himself killed 'cause he took a fool chance with a woman that he wouldn't have had he been up against a man."[6]

"I'll float my stick along with you, may *Ka-Dih*[7] have mercy on me for doing it," the Kid drawled. "Look at all the things Beguinage was pulling at a time both here and down to Brownsville. Unless he had help to do 'em, he'd need to be livelier'n a one-legged man at a butt-kicking contest. Which he couldn't ask for better'n to have a woman for a sidekick. Dressed and acting right, most places she'd draw less notice than a man. And, like Waco said, being a she-male don't make her harmless, or less capable of doing ornery meanness."

"I never said *that*," Waco objected, the banter coming instinctively in spite of his awareness that the situation was extremely serious. "So don't you-all go putting words into my innocent lil mouth, even if I aimed to say 'em and didn't."

"I'll ram my boot into your innocent *big* mouth happen you don't stop horsing around," Dusty warned, although he knew the youngster was taking the matter anything but as lightheartedly as appeared on the surface. "So, happen you've got anything that's useful to say, spill it."

"Thing being," Waco obliged, looking far from abashed by the rebuke. "Happen Beguinage had a woman for a sidekick,

---

5. Told in: THE BAD BUNCH.—*J.T.E.*
6. Told in: THE COW THIEVES.—*J.T.E.*
7. *Ka-Dih*: the "Great Spirit" of the Comanche nation.—*J.T.E.*

they could've been a whole heap closer 'n' more cosy than just two folks earning a living together killing for hire. Which she wouldn't take it kind that you'd gunned her loving man down, Dusty. They do say that sort of thing can rile a gal up a mite when it happens."

"You said that feller you shot at the hotel reckoned they'd been sent there by a woman, Captain Fog," the shipowner commented, having listened to all that was being said and growing increasingly impressed by the shrewd assumptions drawn by the three young Texans.

"Not in so many words," Dusty corrected. "But they came out to mean it."

"Then you think that Beguinage's woman could be trying to take revenge on you, Captain Fog?" the Governor suggested.

"Maybe not just on *me*," the small Texan replied. "She might be fixing to get evens with everybody who she reckons had a hand in him getting killed. That could have been why she made wolf bait of Digbry, unless all she wanted from him was to get back Beguinage's knife and the pot of poison."

"It could've been some of both," Waco pointed out, darting a glance at Liebenfrau and wondering how the revenge theory could have provoked the attack at the livery barn. Drawing no conclusions, he continued, "This being their first time over here from all accounts, she likely wouldn't know where to get any more of that poison. It's not something to come off just any old general store's shelves. And she could've took along the knife to remember him by."

"How would she know Digbry had them?" the shipowner asked.

"The same way she found out that I'd killed him," Dusty supplied. "She was hiding somewhere close by. Not in the warehouse, likely, but got in after we'd left. In that case, when she found his gear was missing, thinking I was just a hired gun, she'd figure as Digbry was a lawman it would be him who'd taken it."

"I'll tell you one thing, though," Waco drawled, indicating the weapon that had ben thrown at the Personal Attendant and lay with the hooked stick on the study's desk. "This knife didn't kill Hoffmeyer, nor one like it."

"Neither did the one Beguinage tried to use on me," Dusty went on, appreciating the point raised by the youngster. "Whatever it was had to be sharp and thin—"

"And something that didn't look dangerous," Waco interjected.

"And which a woman could have in her hand without it looking suspicious," Dusty continued as if the interruption had not occurred.

"A hat pin?" the Governor offered.

"The hole in Digbry's neck was a mite too big for that," Dusty objected.

"How about a knitting needle?" Waco suggested, anticipating his *amigo's* thoughts on the subject.

"Why sure," the Kid put in dryly, despite considering that the youngster's suggestion could be correct. "And he didn't think maybe it was a mite strange that a gal he'd never seen afore'd come sitting on his desk knitting a pair of socks."

"She'd only've been knitting *one* sock," Waco corrected, then made it clear he was addressing his next remarks to everybody except his challenger. "Way I see it, she went to Digbry allowing she'd got something valuable and was scared of having it wide-looped so would the nice, kind marshal look after it for her. And, being the good-hearted gent he was—or 'cause she offered to pay him, which's more likely—he said 'yes' and opened up the drawer. Soon's she saw what she'd come after was in it, she rammed the knitting needle into his neck and that was that."

"What if they hadn't been in the drawer?" Tragg inquired, although he conceded that there was nothing improbable about the theory.

"Then she'd likely've decided that itty-bitty lock didn't look strong enough to guard her valuables and would the marshal put them in his big old iron safe?" Waco deduced, then darted a challenging glare at the Kid. "And, afore this smart-assed yahoo says it, she didn't need to walk in knitting *one* sock. But there wouldn't look to be anything unusual, or suspicious, about a woman taking a knitting needle—not even two—out of her handbag when she was looking for something in it."[8]

"That makes sense to me," Tragg declared and there was a muted rumble of agreement from the other men, in which even the Kid joined. "You'd make a pretty fair lawman, young feller."

"I tried it one time and didn't take to it, there's too much walking," Waco replied, embarrassed by the response his theory had evoked. "So I'm staying clear from now on."[9]

"Hey though," the Kid drawled, knowing his young *amigo* well enough to decide a change of subject would not be unwelcome. "Seeing you're doing all this fancy figuring, how about telling us what this gal of Beguinage's looks like?"

"If she features *you* she'd be an ugly—!" Waco began.

"Which means you don't have a notion," the Kid scoffed. "How about you, Dusty?"

"The feller at the saloon allowed she was a foreigner of some sort, but couldn't guess which country she hailed from except it didn't seem like she was Spanish or Italian," the small Texan replied. "Said she'd mousey brown hair and was a mite prettier than he usually got to work for him. But, having seen the rest of his girls, that doesn't necessarily mean she's out and out beautiful."

"How about her height and build?" Tragg inquired, realizing that in a port like Corpus Christie the fact that the woman might be a foreigner would only be of minimal assistance in locating her unless there was more information.

"About average and nothing special either way," Dusty answered.

"Now, *that's* going to make finding her a whole heap easier," the Kid said sardonically. "I get the feeling good ole Beguinage didn't want to help us any too much."

8. While there is no confirmation in the documents examined by the author, both "Cap" Fog and he believe that the murder was carried out in the manner Waco suggested.—*J.T.E.*

9. New readers can find references to the various volumes which cover Waco's career as a peace officer before and after the events recorded here in Appendix Four.—*J.T.E.*

Before the matter could be discussed further, there was a knock on the door. It was opened at once and Senator Blaby came in followed by a thickset, crop-haired man of Teutonic appearance. Although it had been announced that the reception would be informal because of the prevailing conditions, both wore the correct formal evening attire. It was clear from their expressions that something was wrong. Furthermore, despite knowing that the Governor had wanted to keep the meeting in the study from the other guests' attention, in their haste neither of them thought to close the door behind them.

"I'm sorry to burst in like this, gentlemen," announced Blaby, whose cadaverous face and gaunt build seemed better suited to an undertaker than a politician. "But this is urgent!"

"It's my nephews, Colonel Liebenfrau," the second man went on, his accent that of a well-educated Texan for all of his Germanic cast of features. He was Ludwig von Farlenheim, a successful Brownsville businessman, who had played a prominent part in arranging for Crown Prince Rudolph's visit. "They've had a quarrel and it ended with Fritz challenging Alex to a duel."

"I'll come straight away!" the Personal Attendant barked, almost springing to his feet and advancing with purposeful steps.

"And me!" Tragg declared, having no need for the suggestive glance directed his way by the Governor. "Duelling's against the law in the United States, Colonel. So I'm not having any of it in my bailiwick."

"We may as well go out and join the other guests, gentlemen," Howard suggested, watching the four men passing through a small knot of people who had been looking into the study. "Or do you want to stay out of sight, Captain Fog?"

"There's no point in doing it now I've been seen," Dusty answered, having noticed that Charlene, *Comtesse de* Petain was at the forefront of the group and eyeing him in a speculative fashion. "So I may as well go out and see what's doing."

"If you meet anybody you know," the Governor remarked, standing up, "they might think it's odd that you've changed the colour of your hair."

"Likely they will," the small Texan conceded, with just a suggestion of asperity. "But it'll make a whole lot more talk

should word get out that I've arrived and didn't go to be introduced to the Crown Prince. We'll make out I've just come in
from the OD Connected and I had a message for you from
Uncle Devil. So, when I heard you were in the study, I came
straight there instead of to the ballroom."

"He's sneaky enough to be able to think up a real smart lie
for why his hair's gone black all of a sudden, too," the Kid
informed the shipowner, soberly and holding his voice at exactly the right pitch to sound as if he was imparting confiden-
tial information for the other's ears only, yet making sure that
the subject of the comment—who was walking towards the
door with Howard—also heard. "Ain't he, Waco?"

"No, sir, he's *not*!" the youngster asserted, adopting a self-
righteous tone. "As a true and loyal hand's don't take a kind to
riding the blister end of a shovel 'cause I've riled up my gen-
erous 'n' good-hearted boss, I have to state right out that he
isn't sneaky enough to tell a real *smart* lie about anything."

"I don't suppose you-all need a couple of hands for one of
your boats, do you?" Dusty inquired, pausing and looking
over his shoulder.

"*Those* two?" replied the shipowner, to whom the question
was directed, falling into the spirit of the exchange. "I'd
sooner sink my ships."

"Blast!" Dusty groaned, resuming his interrupted departure. "I was hoping to do the spread a favour and get rid of
them."

"Why, Captain Fog," Charlene greeted, as the small Texan
left the study. She had let the Governor go by so that she could
speak with him. "I see you haven't done anything about your
hair."

"No, ma'am," Dusty replied, watching Liebenfrau and the
sheriff going through a door at the other side of the ballroom.
Then he returned his gaze to the *Comtesse*. She was wearing a
pale green ball gown which left little to be imagined about the
rich contours of her figure and her bearing was regal. "I found
that this double-dam—awful dye just wouldn't wash away
like I was promised. So I came along hoping nobody would
notice I'm not a blond any more." He paused as he glanced at
the buffet table, then ejaculated, "Whooee! Man oh man!
Who-all's that right pretty lil gal talking to Mark?"

"An English wom—*lady*—who has attached her—been invited to come to the United States with Rud—His Highness," Charlene answered and her antipathy would have been obvious even to a person less perceptive than the small Texan.

"So that's *her*, huh?" Dusty drawled, showing nothing to suggest he had already had the Lady pointed out to him and shared his companions' misgivings where she was concerned. "Old Liebenfrau's not too taken with the notion, but I can see why the Prince has asked her to go on the hunt with us."

"Asked *her*?" the *Comtesse* repeated, glaring viciously at the blonde and clearly far from pleased by the prospect. Then she shrugged and went on, "I shouldn't think she accepted. These Englishwomen don't do anything so strenuous as that."

"So I've always heard," Dusty drawled, thinking of the strenuous activities in which he had known one Englishwoman to indulge. "Excuse me, ma'am. I'd best go over and present myself to Her Ladyship. I know a couple of folks from England and I reckon she might too."

A scowl flickered across Charlene's face as the small Texan walked away. She had hoped to persuade the Crown Prince to include her in the party, the assassination plot required that she should go on it. Wondering if Dusty might have been misinformed, she decided to follow him and make a closer acquaintance with the blonde. Her intentions were frustrated by the Kid and Waco. Guessing what their *amigo* was going to do, they were determined that nothing would stop him. So they converged upon the *Comtesse* and introduced her to the shipowner, employing such formality that it was impossible for her to walk away immediately without giving offence.

CHAPTER ELEVEN

I Know Who You're *Not*

"Lady Winifred, allow me to present my *amigo*, Captain Dusty Fog," Mark Counter said, as the small Texan strolled up. "Dusty, this is Lady Winifred Amelia Besgrove-Woodstole."

"My pleasure, ma'am," Dusty drawled, deciding that he was addressing one of the two most beautiful women in the room and conceding that, even though he had grave doubts about her, she had a far greater appeal to his aesthetic tastes than Charlene, *Comtesse de* Petain.

"Enchanted," the Lady replied and, in spite of her warm, friendly smile, there was a wary glint in her eyes. "This is a pleasure, Captain Fog. I've heard so much about you."

Mark had arrived with Major the Baron von Goeringwald, Captain Fritz von Farlenheim and their men, while the examination of Hoffmeyer's body was being carried out, having been directed to the scene by the Lady's maid. At the blond giant's suggestion, the First Taster and an orderly had remained with the body. Waco had been sent to inform the town marshal of what had happened, obtaining a similar reply to that given to the bell boy from the Portside Hotel, while the rest of the party continued to their destination.

In the absence of instructions to the contrary, the Lady's baggage had been delivered from the U.S.S. *Nantucket* on its arrival along with that of Crown Prince Rudolph and his retinue. Despite already having Governor Stanton Howard, some of his staff and the *Comtesse* as guests at the mansion, Mrs. Blaby had shown no hesitation over providing accommodation for the beautiful young Englishwoman. Not only had she considered it a considerable boost socially to have yet another member of the European aristocracy on the premises, she found that she would have the services of a second trained maid to help at the reception.

Having learned from Florence Drakefield that she had a rival for the royal visitor's favours, the Lady had made her preparations for attending the reception accordingly. The maid had shown how speedily a servant could obtain information. Not only had she heard something of the day's events in Corpus Christie and passed them on to her employer, she had discovered what the *Comtésse* would be wearing and how it would be regarded by the other female guests. Using the latter as a guide, the Lady had selected an ensemble which she believed would serve as a perfect counterfoil. Her judgement had proved to be correct. Whereas Charlene's attire bordered on the *risqué*, at least by local standards, her own decorous white ball gown and its accoutrements had clearly met with unanimous approval by Mrs. Blaby and the local ladies. Nor had its modest lines detracted from her beauty, or lessened the interest shown towards her by the male guests.

When the Lady had been told by her maid that there was a meeting taking place in her host's study, and that the servants had received orders to stay out until it was over, she had made a shrewd guess what had brought it about. She had also wished that she could have heard what was being said. Although it was rumoured that one of three would-be killers who had died earlier that day was a notorious European professional assassin, the way in which Hoffmeyer had been done to death convinced her it could not have been Beguinage. Accepting that eavesdropping by herself or Florence would be too risky, she had hoped to find out if Mark knew anything. The argument between the von Farlenheim cousins had prevented her from making any progress. And despite her being presented with what on the surface appeared to be an opportunity to obtain information from the small Texan—who had come from the study although there had been no mention that he was even in the mansion—it did not produce the result she required.

"Oh ho!" Mark drawled, glancing across the ballroom. "From the look of things, I'd best go and rescue the *Comtésse* from those two varmints. If you'll excuse me, ma'am."

"Of course," the Lady authorized, having noticed that

Charlene was glowering in her direction and was clearly annoyed at being held in conversation by the Ysabel Kid, Waco and the well-dressed man. As Mark walked away, she returned her gaze to the small Texan. "Have you met the *Comtesse*, Captain Fog?"

"Hey, it is *you*, Cap'n Fog!" a voice announced, before Dusty could reply. "Only I allus thought you'd got white hair!"

Looking around, the small Texan found that one of the cattlemen who had prevented him from following the anarchist "Gotz" from the Portside Hotel was approaching. From a slight unsteadiness in his gait and his tone, it appeared that he had drunk just a little too much and was in a convivial mood.

"I'm not *that* old," Dusty answered, hoping the conversation would not be protracted.

"No offence," the man apologized, teetering to a stop. "I didn't know you was in Corpus Christie, or I'd've looked you up."

"I've not long since come in," Dusty replied. "Do you want to see me about anything special?"

"*You* might call it *that*," the man stated, with a conspiratorial grin. "I've just come down from Mulrooney and Freddie Woods said I should tell you-all, 'Howdy' should I see you when I got back to Texas. Now *there's* a for-real fine lady, Cap'n Fog. And isn't that lil blonde gal of her's, Babsy, a pistol?"

"She sure is," Dusty agreed coldly, having seen that the Lady stiffened slightly on hearing the name of the person who had sent the message from Mulrooney.

"Yes, sir, those two English gals aren't nothing like I've always heard—" the cattleman continued, then began to realize that there was a lack of cordiality in the way the Lady and the small Texan were regarding him. Remembering what he had been told about her place of origin, he drew an erroneous conclusion over the cause of the chilly response. So, letting his words trail off, he finished apologetically, "Well, I reckon I'd best go and find the missus. It's been nice talking with you-all, ma'am, Cap'n Fog."

"I hope your friend's wife doesn't disapprove of him taking a drink or two," the Lady remarked, as the man walked away more quickly than he had approached. For all her amiable exterior, she gave just a hint of uneasiness and concern. "For my part, I don't care, unless it is done to the point where it makes a person obnoxious and he certainly wasn't."

"No, ma'am," Dusty answered noncommittally. "Shall we go into the garden so that we can talk privately?"

"Why Captain Fog!" the Lady gasped, trying to sound shocked yet overtly pleased by the suggestion. She was aware that—despite the polite way in which the proposal had been uttered—it was a command rather than a request, but she believed that she might profit from it. "That might be considered *very* forward of you. Or would such a thing be considered proper in Texas so soon after we were introduced?"

"You said that very well, ma'am," Dusty drawled, then his tone hardened as he went on, "But, even if you *really* cared, it's 'proper' enough for what we have to talk about. Fact being, I reckon *you'd* prefer it that way."

"Now you've intrigued me, although I can't *imagine* what you mean," the Lady answered, trying to sound more carefree than she was feeling. Impressed by the strength of the small Texan's personality, she realized that he could not be judged by the criteria of mere feet and inches. Competent and intelligent as she had found his three companions, she sensed that he was even more so. Furthermore, she appreciated that—as the contingency she had dismissed earlier as inconceivable now appeared to be correct—she was in no position to ignore his wishes. Catching her maid's eye as the latter was offering the only glass on a tray to another of the guests, she gave a slight motion with her head and received just as barely a perceptible nod to indicate her signal had been understood. Managing a smile, she went on, "Shall we go, Captain?"

"It'll be my pleasure, ma'am," the small Texan conceded, accepting the arm offered by the Englishwoman. "I reckon we'll be through before His Highness comes down."

"I hope so," the Lady replied. "It really wasn't very tactful of your friend to have allowed His Highness to go after that stag instead of coming straight here."

"Tact's never been a thing Lon was strong on," Dusty admitted with a grin, although he had earlier expressed his own feelings on the Ysabel Kid's behaviour in allowing the royal visitor to hunt and collect an exceptionally fine buck whitetail deer they had come across on the way from the rendezvous. "But His Highness enjoyed it and took a better than fair trophy, even if doing it made them late in arriving."

To all appearances, as they walked side by side across the room and through the open french windows, the Lady and the small Texan might have been on the best of terms. However, even before they had disappeared into the mansion's grounds, Florence Drakefield was carrying her tray towards the door of the kitchen.

"All right, ma'am," Dusty said, after he had allowed the blonde to guide him in silence until they were partially concealed among the decorative bushes at the right side of the mansion. "Just who are you?"

"You know who I am," the Lady objected, although her voice held little conviction, disengaging her arm from the small Texan's hand and moving until she stood in front of him. "So why—?"

"No, ma'am, I know who you're *not*," Dusty corrected. "So why don't you quit wasting both our time and tell me who you really are?"

"I don't understand!" the Lady protested, glancing around as if to make sure there was nobody close by and making nervous-seeming gestures with her hands until the right one was hidden behind her. "Would you care to explain before I go back inside and complain about your strange behaviour to Senator Blaby?"

"You're not Lady Winifred Amelia Besgrove-Woodstole," Dusty stated and his attitude left it obvious that he would accept no denial.

"If that is meant to be a practical joke—!" the Lady began, playing for the time her maid would need to locate them.

"You *know* it's not," Dusty declared. "Fact being, you heard enough back there to let you know that Lady Winifred's up in Mulrooney, Kansas, living under the name of 'Freddie Woods.'"

"Now isn't that *infuriating*?" the Lady sighed, speaking with well simulated exasperation, but standing as tense and defensive as a bobcat confronted by a hound dog. "I thought I would be safe using Freddie's name. The butler and other servants at her people's country house told me she was paying an extended visit to one of the family in Ceylon."

"There's times you just can't depend on *anybody*," Dusty drawled, but there was no sympathy in his voice. "Take your maid, for instance. Don't count on her sneaking up on me. I saw you wig-wagging to her, so it won't come off."

"Why not?" the Lady inquired, assailed by the bitter knowledge that her strategy had failed and nursing the worrying conviction that it was also being countered.

"Lon's close by and he'll copper any bets she tries to put down," the small Texan explained. "Aren't you, *amigo*?"

"Why sure," replied the voice of the Ysabel Kid, imbued with such a ventriloquial quality that his exact location could not be determined. "Tell you what though, ma'am, that gal of your'n's pretty good. She's near to here already."

"It's all right, Florence," the Lady called, seeing the maid appear from behind a bush and stare around, trying to find the speaker. "You can go back indoors."

"Yes, Mi—Your Ladyship," Florence answered. "If that's what *you* want."

"It isn't," the Lady admitted with a wry smile. "But we haven't any other choice." After the maid had carried out her instructions by departing, she swung her gaze to the small Texan. "I don't suppose you'd send Lon away, so I won't ask you to pretend to."

"Lady," the Kid's voice answered, but it did not supply any suggestion as to where he was speaking from. "Happen Dusty told me—and meant it—I'd go."

"I believe you, even though I know I wouldn't be able to tell whether you'd gone or were still there," the Lady replied. "So we may as well get down to what has brought us out here, Captain Fog."

"Why sure, ma'am," Dusty obliged, but his lazy drawl had an edge of steel in its timbre. "Who are you and what're you up to?"

"What if I tell you that neither is any of your business?" the Lady challenged, her air of defiance mingled with a sense of realization that it was futile.

"The jail in town's not what I'd call comfortable," Dusty warned. "And you could find the girls you'll be sharing your cell with aren't the most friendly, or gentle, company."

"'Specially was they to be given the notion things'd go easier for 'em happen they treated you mean," the Kid supplemented.

"You'll have to charge me with something before you could put me there!" the Lady protested, trying to keep any trace of anxiety from her voice. "I'm a British subject and our Government would take the most grave exception if they heard that I'd been imprisoned for no reason."

"You're using an English lady from a real important family's name," Dusty pointed out, although he was aware that Great Britain was such an important country few other nations would deliberately incur its wrath. "Which's good enough cause for us to hold you. And, way Congress feels about keeping the Crown Prince safe while he's over here, they'd back us to the hilt *if* your Government heard and complained about us holding you."

"*If* they heard?" the Lady repeated. "Do you mean that I could be held incommunicado?"

"Could be," Dusty admitted.

"You wouldn't dare!" the Lady snapped, trying to sound more certain than she felt.

"Don't count on it," Dusty replied. "Anyways, there wouldn't be the need for us to do it. Your own police'll likely be wanting to know why you tricked the Crown Prince into thinking you're Lady Winifred Besgrove-Woodstole and I'd be willing to bet that your Government are just as eager as Congress to make sure nothing happens to him. So which is it to be, talk to me or stay in jail until we find out what they want us to do?"

"Wouldn't want you to take this into account one way or the other, ma'am," the Kid put in, his voice seeming to change from point to point as the words continued. "But it'll be lil ole *me* who takes you to the pokey. I'm not all white like Dusty, Mark 'n' Waco, a fair piece of me's Comanche. Way us *Nemenuh*—which's Comanch' for 'The People' and our name for us—figure it, a woman's only a mite more use than a feed-dog. Fact being, she's near's useful as a mule, but not close to's valuable as a good hoss or a repeating rifle. So we're not over-choosey how we treat you gals. Which *I'd* be real riled happen you-all didn't tell me everything Dusty wants to know."

"What a charming outlook," the Lady said, restraining a shudder at the gentle yet frightening way in which the unseen Texan had spoken. Wondering if the threat would be carried out, she decided it might be if necessary. So, considering that her only hope was to be at least acceptably frank, she yielded to the inevitable. Exerting all her willpower to speak confidently, she went on, "My name is Amelia Benkinsop and I assure you I wouldn't do anything to harm Crown Prince Rudolph. In fact, I came with him to try to prevent him from being killed."

"No offence, ma'am," Dusty said, wondering if the blonde's attitude of sincerity was genuine. "But I'd be obliged if you'd bring your right hand out where I can see it's empty. And, although I'm not from Missouri—"

"You have to be shown," the Lady interrupted, doing as she was asked and leaving the Remington Double Derringer she had been grasping in its carefully concealed pocket at the rear of the gown. "I've heard the saying. Rudolph saved my life one night in Paris and I *never* forget a debt. Besides—"

"Go on," Dusty prompted, detecting nothing to suggest the blonde was lying.

"I've another reason for coming to your country. As Waco undoubtedly told you, Beguinage killed my uncle. He meant a lot to me and had done a lot for me. As I said, I *always* honour my obligations."

"So you figure on getting Beguinage to avenge him?"

"I suppose you think a mere woman wouldn't be capable of doing it?" the Lady demanded indignantly.

"Ma'am," Dusty drawled. "Even afore I met Freddie Woods, who's a real remarkable lady happen you don't know it, I'd learned it *never* pays to sell a woman short. But you've had a long boat ride for nothing. Beguinage is dead."

"Dead?" Amelia gasped.

"I killed him this morning," Dusty elaborated.

"I hadn't heard about it!"

"The marshal covered up for me by reckoning somebody else had done it."

"You mean that he was one of the three men who died this

morning?" Amelia asked. "But *none* of them could have been Beguinage!"

"Why not?" Dusty demanded.

"I told you that he murdered my uncle," the Lady explained. "Hoffmeyer was killed in exactly the same way, even to having an identical hole in the side of his throat and the hideous expression on his face."

"And so was the marshal," Dusty pointed out.

"I've heard that he was kill—!" Amelia commenced, then realized the full import of the small Texan's words. "You mean that he died in the same way as Hoffmeyer?"

"I haven't seen Hoffmeyer's body," Dusty confessed. "But from the way Waco described it, the same thing had killed them both."

"You said the marshal had helped you to—cover up?—that it was you who killed Beguinage."

"He did."

"In that case," the Lady asked. "How could he have been killed by Beguinage, who was already dead?"

"We figure it was his woman who killed the marshal and Hoffmeyer," Dusty replied, wishing there was more light so that he could form a better impression of the reaction to his words.

"His *woman*?" Amelia breathed, slapping her right hand against her thigh in a gesture of exasperation. "Of *course*! That would explain so many things."

"Such as how Beguinage managed to get to your uncle?" Dusty suggested.

"How did you guess?" Amelia gasped.

"We figured it would've had to be a woman who could get close enough to the marshal," Dusty replied. "He'd never have trusted a man."

"Uncle Marcel always had an eye for the ladies," Amelia said thoughtfully. "And, although I've never heard so much as a hint that Beguinage worked other than alone, I did wonder how he achieved some of his successes without help. Not that *anybody* would admit to knowing much more than that Beguinage existed, even those through whom he could be reached with offers of employment."

"Did you reckon anybody would admit any more to you?"

Dusty inquired, puzzled by the way in which the Lady had spoken. It conveyed the impression that she was surprised more positive information had failed to materialize.

"I did," Amelia stated, realizing that she had said too much and, dealing with such a shrewd and discerning person, she could not hope to bluff her way clear. "Mostly there is little that goes on in criminal circles, especially at such a high level, that one can't learn at least some of the details if one knows who and where to ask."

"And *you* know who 'n' where?" the Kid asked, from his still concealed location.

"I do," Amelia declared. "My family have long had connections with many of Europe's leading international criminals."[1]

"You're an owlhoot?" the Kid drawled, sounding disbelieving.

"Nothing has ever been proven," Amelia answered primly.

"We had us a run in with one of them leading international criminals from Europe a piece back," the Kid remarked, advancing to the Lady's side from the opposite direction to where she had thought him to be. "Can't just bring his name to mind, but he was so took by me that he gave me a right fancy pocket-knife."

"It was the Ox," Amelia declared, knowing she was being subjected to a test. "His full name is Octavius Xavier Guillemot[2] and he is, not to put too fine a point on it, very fat. He must have been taken with you to part with *that* knife. I'm surprised he didn't try to enlist you in his search for that Crusaders' bird he's always talking about."[3]

"Was some talk of it," the Kid conceded, accepting that the beautiful Englishwoman was speaking the truth about her fam-

---

1. The Benkinsop family has retained its close connections with the leading members of international criminal circles, as is told in: BLONDE GENIUS.—*J.T.E.*

2. The events which involved the Ysabel Kid with Octavius Xavier "the Ox" Guillemot are told in: THE QUEST FOR BOWIE'S BLADE.—*J.T.E.*

3. Details of another man's search for the "Crusaders' bird" are given in: THE MALTESE FALCON BY Dashiell Hammet.—*J.T.E.*

ily connections. "But I didn't cotton to the notion of going riding on a boat."

"How much do you know about Beguinage?" Dusty asked and the Lady decided that she had convinced the Texans of her veracity.

"Very little, as I said," Amelia replied. "He has such a well-run system that it's impossible to follow the chain by which he receives requests to take employment. It was more of a guess, or hope that he had been hired, that caused me to renew my friendship with Prince Rudolph. That and wanting to help protect him."

"You knew that somebody was after his hide?" Dusty inquired.

"Yes, that much I managed to find out," Amelia admitted. "And as I was told that Beguinage would not be available for three months at least, I assumed he was hired to assassinate His Highness."

"I don't suppose you know who hired him?" Dusty said, more as a statement than a question.

"I'm afraid not," the Lady sighed. "It could be either the Council of Noble Birth, or the anarchists. As you probably know, both factions are hoping to bring about His Highness' death. Until tonight, if I'd had to pick between them, I would have said the Council. They're all Bosgravnian nobles and would have sufficient money to meet Beguinage's fee."

"What happened tonight to make you change your mind?" Dusty wanted to know.

"I found out that the *Comtesse de* Petain is here," Amelia replied.

"Do you know her?" the small Texan inquired.

"We hadn't met until Mrs. Blaby introduced us," the Lady answered, in a voice which suggested a deep dislike for the French aristocrat. "But I've heard about her and none of it was good."

"And you reckon that she's here to assassinate His Highness?"

"You said *that* as if the idea hadn't already occurred to you, Captain Fog," Amelia chided with a smile. "She's either here to help assassinate His Highness, or to do it herself. Do you think she might be Beguinage's woman?"

"If she is, it wasn't her who killed the marshal, or Hoffmeyer," Dusty replied. "She hasn't been out of somebody or other's sight since well before Digbry was killed. I've checked on that."

"I thought you would have," Amelia admitted. "However, the Council wouldn't have hired them both. One of the few things I learned was that Beguinage will not countenance any opposition when he's accepted an assignment. He's warned off, or killed, other assassins who have threatened to trespass upon his tasks."

"Captain Fog!" called a feminine voice the Lady and the Texans recognized.

"They do say if you talk of the devil, he shows up," the Kid commented, looking in the speaker's direction.

"We're here, *Comtesse*," Dusty replied, making a gesture with his head that caused his *amigo* to disappear silently. Taking Amelia's arm, he walked with her to meet the other woman. "Do you know Lady Winifred?"

"We've been introduced," Charlene answered, trying to sound disinterested. "Rud—His Highness has joined the company. So Mark and I came to look for you as we felt you would wish to be presented."

"Trust good old Mark to think of that," Dusty drawled, although he was confident the suggestion had not come from the blond giant. "Have *you-all* been presented to His Highness, ma'am?"

"It is hardly necessary," Charlene replied with a touch of hauteur, the question having been directed at her.

"Well I'll swan, that's right. You have!" Dusty declared. "How'd I ever come to forget when I was telling you that Lady Winifred's coming on the hunt with you?"

"Forget what?" Charlene demanded.

"When His Highness heard you were in Corpus Christie," the small Texan answered, "he straight off told Mark that he is going to ask you if you'd like to go along with us as well."

CHAPTER TWELVE

Or Should I Say *"DUSTY FOG"*?

"You are punctual, Mr. Clint," commented the anarchist who had called himself "Gotz," holding open the front door of the house he had nominated for the meeting and standing aside to allow the small Texan to enter. "Please come in quickly to make sure that nobody knows we are here."

In Dusty Fog's opinion, most of the day's events had been progressing in a generally satisfactory manner.

On returning to the ballroom of Senator Blaby's mansion, accompanied by Amelia Benkinsop and Charlene, *Comtesse de* Petain, Dusty had had his first meeting with Crown Prince Rudolph of Bosgravnia. They had taken an instant liking to one another. In the small Texan's case, it had been enhanced by the way in which the royal visitor had reacted when the *Comtesse* thanked him for the invitation to join the hunting party. Nothing in his response had suggested that this was the first he had heard of the matter. Nor had she learned differently when speaking with the other men who would be involved.

Moving swiftly and unnoticed by either of the women, the Ysabel Kid had been in the ballroom before they arrived and had warned Mark Counter and Waco what to expect. Colonel Wilhelm Liebenfrau, Major the Baron von Goeringwald and Captain Fritz von Farlenheim were absent until later. By the time they were available for Charlene to speak with them, they had been informed that she and Amelia would be accompanying them and received the Crown Prince's orders to confirm that it had been his decision if questioned by anybody.

Another pleasing facet of Rudolph's character had been displayed shortly after Dusty was presented to him. Claiming that they felt out of place in such "fancy" company, the Kid and Waco had asked permission to leave. They had said that

119

they preferred to spend their leisure time in the part of Corpus Christie resembling the areas in which they usually found their entertainment and relaxation. When the small Texan had displayed reluctance over giving permission, the Crown Prince had interceded on their behalf. Pointing out that the Kid had already helped him to acquire a fine trophy, he had used his influence to produce a change of mind on Dusty's part. What was more, he had insisted, against the small Texan's advice, in rewarding the Kid handsomely. The two OD Connected hands had taken their departure with a warning from their segundo to stay sober and keep out of trouble. It had been clear to the onlookers that neither had been pleased by the restrictions which were being placed on their activities. Also that Dusty did not approve of them going.

On Liebenfrau's orders, Fritz and Alex von Farlenheim had been kept separated while the cause of the quarrel was investigated. All the evidence had indicated that the latter was to blame and had provoked his cousin. It had been decided by the Personal Attendant and their uncle that Alex should leave Corpus Christie in the interest of avoiding any repetition of the incident. There had been no delay in putting the decision into effect. Ludwig von Farlenheim had known the captain of a ship which was leaving for Brownsville that night and Alex, who had clearly bitterly resented the order, was instructed to be aboard when it sailed. Sheriff Elvis Tragg had accompanied Ludwig to ensure that the young man did not disobey, then had gone to take charge of investigating the murders of Town Marshal Benjamin Digbry and Liebenfrau's orderly.

Throughout the evening, it had been obvious to Dusty that Charlene did not intend missing anything, nor would she allow Amelia an opportunity to be alone with the Crown Prince. Although the two beautiful women had been icily polite to each other, there was clearly no love lost between them.

One of the things learned by the small Texan as the evening had progressed was what Fritz von Farlenheim's duties as "First Taster" entailed. Originally, the holder of the office had been required to eat a portion of every dish and test every drink presented to his ruler. Of recent years, it had come to be considered sufficient for him to open and serve the Crown Prince's liquid refreshments. When Dusty had remarked that such a situation could be exploited by would-be assassins, Liebenfrau had stated that the young captain's loyalty and devotion to their ruler was unquestioned. He had also declared that he was satisfied no harm would ever befall Rudolph as a result of drinks being tampered with as long as Fritz carried out the von Farlenheim family's tradition by serving as First Taster.

Apart from having seen Alex von Farlenheim depart, there had been little positive news for the sheriff to report when he returned at ten o'clock. On his arrival at the town marshal's office, he had found it deserted. He had learned that, after the removal of Digbry's body, all the deputies had disappeared. Faced with the possibility of their various illicit activities being brought to light during an investigation into the murder, they had made the most of their opportunities and fled. Having no other assistance, Tragg had been unable to make any progress in the task of locating the killer.

The sheriff's final piece of news was such that Dusty might have preferred to hear it in private. Instead, it had been delivered where the royal visitor and the other guests could hear. Finding the Kid and Waco much the worse for drink as a result of Rudolph's largesse, Tragg stated that he had considered it advisable to take them to jail. As such behaviour was far from uncommon when cowhands found themselves in similar conditions of affluence, few of the crowd had been surprised to hear what had happened. Dusty had expressed his annoyance. Nor was he noticeably mollified to learn that the errant pair had done no damage and would be released in the morning.

Claiming that he was tired after the hurried journey he had made so as to arrive in time for the reception, the small Texan had asked for and been granted permission to retire at a quarter after ten. Leaving Mark to keep watch on Amelia and Charlene, he set off ostensibly to the hotel in which the other members of the floating outfit had taken rooms. His actual destination had been the house to which he had been directed by "Gotz's" letter.

Dusty had not forgotten that, assuming the theory formulated in Blaby's study was correct, Beguinage's female accomplice was still at liberty. Although the men who were hired to kill him at the Portside Hotel had failed, he felt sure that she had not abandoned her desire to be avenged. So he had put into practise the methods he had employed when walking the rounds as a peace officer in a less than law-abiding section of a town. By doing so, he had made himself a far from easy target should any ambush be planned. None had materialized, but he did not regret having taken the precautions.

As Dusty had guessed would be the case, the house to which he had been summoned had been carefully selected for its purpose. Small, one storey and dilapidated, it was situated in what was now a derelict part of town. There was no other building within at least a hundred yards on any side. Even on such a moderately dark night, it would be almost impossible to approach unseen provided the occupants were keeping a watch.

The house was in complete darkness and was, apparently, as deserted as the other buildings in the vicinity appeared to be. However, when "Gotz" opened the front door in answer to the small Texan's knock, he found why there was no outward signs of occupancy. A lantern glowed feebly on a rickety table in the centre of the room, but its faint illumination was prevented from showing outside by thick blankets hanging over the windows.

"Why sure, just as soon's you've backed off towards the table," Dusty replied to the invitation to enter, noticing that the bearded anarchist seemed to be the only other person present. "It's not that I don't trust you-all behind me, but like I told you at the hotel, I'm a cautious sort of a feller."

"Whatever you wish," "Gotz" answered, withdrawing as requested and watching his visitor advance across the threshold. "But hurry, please. You know it is best that *nobody* sees we are here."

On entering, alert for any possible treachery although he had no reason to suspect such was "Gotz's" intention, Dusty's attention was distracted from the anarchist to a door at the other side of the room. It began to move, but the lantern's light was insufficient for him to see who was opening it.

Watching the dark shape taking form at the door across the room, Dusty sensed rather than saw or heard a movement to his left. Then the door through which he had entered began to close behind him and he realized that it was not of its own volition. Before he could look in either direction, two men converged upon him from the rear and seized him by the arms with powerful hands.

"Wha—?" the small Texan began, restraining his first impulse to struggle as he felt the strength by which he was grasped.

"Welcome, Mr. '*Rapido* Clint,'" said the dark shape which was emerging out of the blackness of the other room, its voice feminine, mocking, and with a pronounced French accent. "Or should I say '*Dusty Fog*'?"

"God damn it, 'Gotz'!" the small Texan barked allowing himself to be hustled forward by his captors and watching the speaker walk into the light. Slightly taller than himself, as far as could be discovered, she was on the dumpy side under the hooded cloak which covered her from head to foot. Her face was covered by a black veil and she carried a short-barrelled Webley Royal Irish Constabulary revolver in her right hand. "If this's supposed to try me out for your—!"

"It is no use, *Captain* Fog," the woman stated, before the bearded anarchist could reply. "I know you, even if you don't know me."

"Like hell I don't know you," Dusty answered, as the men brought him to a halt by the table. "I just hope the *Comtesse* won't be riled over you sneaking off when you should be serving your *betters* at the reception."

"*Betters*!" the woman repeated, her whole bearing indicating that the word was one for which she did not care. "Those grasping capitalist—!" The words trailed away as she realized what the comment that had provoked them implied and her voice rose a trifle as she continued, "How did you know *me*?"

"Your *helper* there told me," Dusty replied, nodding to where "Gotz" had retreated and was standing.

"I'm not her—!" the bearded anarchist protested, having the kind of mentality which revolted at the suggestion that he was inferior to anybody else, especially a woman.

"It was only a lucky guess," the woman put in, drawing aside the veil to reveal she was Charlene's maid.

"Shucks no," Dusty objected, the interruption having prevented "Gotz" from acting in the way he had hoped, "I can always recognize a *servant*."

"Soon there will be no *servants*!" the maid spat out, but she too failed to respond in the manner that the small Texan needed. "You won't be alive to see the day, be assured of that!" Then, making an obvious effort, she regained control of herself and looked at "Gotz." "I will go back now, before I'm missed."

While the conversation had been taking place, Dusty had been studying the men who were holding his arms. They were big, well made, brutal-featured and, apart from each having a revolver thrust into his waist belt, dressed after the fashion of ordinary sailors from a merchant ship. A glance downwards had informed him of how they had approached so quietly. Their feet were bare. However, his judgement of the situation warned him that the time was not yet ripe for an attempt to free himself.

"My hired help'll have something to say about *that*," Dusty warned.

"Much *any* of them care what happens to *you*," the maid sniffed, as "Gotz" darted a challenging look at her. "Two of them have been arrested for being drunk and the other is besotted by that aristocratic bitch who treats *me* like a slave. See he doesn't die too quickly and throw his body into the sea. I wish it could be given to the pigs."

"Whee-doggie!" Dusty ejaculated, watching the woman walking past in the direction of the front door. "Now there's one good reason I don't reckon I'd care for the brave new world you-all figuring to give the poor folks."

"What is?" "Gotz" asked, puzzled in spite of himself.

"I'd sure hate to have to take orders from a *woman*," the small Texan explained.

"No *woman* gives orders to *me*!" the anarchist spat out.

"It sure didn't sound like you-all was giving them to *her*," Dusty scoffed and, watching the anger that suffused the bearded face, he pressed onwards with his plan. "Not that I reckoned you'd have much truck with women, being what you are."

"What I am?" "Gotz" came back, frowning with a lack of understanding.

"Way I've always heard it," Dusty said slowly, "your kind would rather have boys than girls."

"What do you mean?" the anarchist demanded, glancing to where the maid was starting to open the front door.

"Come on now," the small Texan drawled, his voice oozing contempt. "I don't know what folks call your kind of scum where you-all come from, but over here the name's a 'swish.'"

A snarl burst from "Gotz." He had spent sufficient time in the United States to have discovered that the word "swish" was the derogatory name for homosexual. While aware that a number of his liberal intellectual associates qualified the term, he felt nothing except revulsion for such an aberration. So he bitterly resented the implication that he indulged in such a practice, particularly when it came from a person of so insignificant an appearance.

"You'll soon find out whether I hit like a 'swish'!" the anarchist bellowed, drawing back his right arm and stepping towards the cause of his wrath.

"Mon dieu!" the maid croaked, staring out of the house as she was about to emerge. Jumping backwards, her voice rose to a terrified shriek and she slammed the door. "His men are coming!"

With his bunched fist driving out, "Gotz" was distracted by the woman's warning. In spite of realizing the danger, he could not halt his actions. Unable to understand much more English than the basic words of command issued when working on a ship, the two men holding Dusty were startled by the commotion without knowing what the maid had said. So, although they started to look around and relaxed their holds a trifle, neither offered to release the captive.

Slight though the reduction of the restraint upon him might be, it gave the small Texan the opportunity for which he had been waiting. What was more, his mocking comments to "Gotz" had produced the kind of response he had hoped for. The woman's participation was an added bonus, although he was by no means surprised to discover that assistance was so close at hand.

The sheriff had been willing to co-operate when he had heard Dusty's proposals for dealing with the anarchists. The maid had all the contempt that most middle-class liberals had for the genuine working classes and she had not doubted that the two cowhands, who were now approaching the house, had behaved in such a manner that the sheriff had had to arrest them. Having Waco and the Kid follow close enough to be able to intervene, instead of walking with him, had been one of the precautions the small Texan had taken against an ambush by Beguinage's woman. There were two extra pairs of keen and unsuspected eyes helping to keep watch for trouble. However, as there was no cover for them between the nearest buildings and the house, they had not attempted to approach until he was inside and holding the attention of the occupants.

Taking advantage of the loosening of his captors' grips, Dusty rolled his head aside and caused "Gotz's" fist to pass without touching him. At the same moment, he snapped up and bent his left leg. Carried onwards by the impetus of the abortive blow, the anarchist received the small Texan's knee just below his breast bone. For all that, he might have counted himself fortunate. The attack was intended to strike his testicles, but had been mistimed slightly. While the impact hurt and sent him staggering backwards for several steps, he was far from incapacitated.

Paying only the scantiest attention to what the men were doing, the maid dashed across the room. Beyond hoping that her companions could cause a sufficient delay to let her make good her escape, she gave no thought to what might happen to them. Once she was outside, she could seek refuge at the home of a sympathizer until a way could be found for her to flee the country. As a precaution, she was carrying the means to blackmail the local anarchist into doing as she desired.

Passing through the second door, a frightening thought struck the woman. She realized that she had seen only two of the small Texan's companions approaching and wondered where the third might be. Even as she remembered that he had still been at the reception when she left to warn her companions of "*Rapido* Clint's" true identity, the memory gave her no comfort. There might be other men surrounding the building. Drawing the hammer of the Webley to fully cocked, regardless that its double-action mechanism rendered this unnecessary, she swore that she would kill anybody who came between her and freedom.

Feeling Dusty's movements, the two men obeyed their instincts and tightened the grips on his arms. By doing so, they were inadvertently playing into his hands. Braced by them and allowing them to support his weight, he raised both legs and brought them down hard. Due to the haste that was necessary if the next part of his plan was to succeed, he achieved only part of his purpose. Descending, the heel of his left boot landed far from gently on the near side man's right toes. The other missed its mark, coming down between the feet of the man at the right. So, although the stricken captor gave a howl of agony, let go, and staggered away, his companion still clung on.

Seeing that "Gotz" was not collapsing and—while still being propelled backwards—was already dipping his right hand into the pocket of his pea-jacket, the small Texan realized the knee had failed to produce the desired result. He also appreciated that there must be no delay in ridding himself of all restraint. In spite of the pain caused by the stamp on his bare foot and the blood oozing from split open toenails, the first of the captors also had not fallen and was clawing at the revolver in his waist belt. The move lacked the cohesive purpose of a highly competent gun-fighter, but it was sufficiently swift to pose a dangerous threat. Nor dare Dusty reply upon the Kid and Waco arriving soon enough to remove it. There was too much noise in the room for him to hear their approaching footsteps and he did not know how far away they had been when seen by the woman.

Bearing that thought in mind, Dusty gave a surging heave with his right shoulder. Already somewhat off balance due to his sudden change from submissively passive to *very* active, the man holding him was not prepared for such a response. Furthermore, the great strength his powerfully muscled small frame was capable of exerting came as a complete surprise.

Almost lifted from his feet, the man felt the arm wrenched from his grasp as he was flung aside.

Alarmed by the apparent ease with which the diminutive Texan was escaping from the clutches of two larger, heavier men, both of whom he knew to be very strong, "Gotz" managed to come to a halt. He was already grasping the butt of his Colt Storekeeper Model Peacemaker, but decided against trying to lift it from the pocket. Instead, jerking back the hammer, he tilted the barrel forward and fired through the thick woollen cloth of the pea-jacket.

Hearing the shot as she was opening the back foor, the maid neither paused nor looked back. Stepping from the house, she found herself confronted by a dark human shape. While unable to discern who it might be, she saw the figure's right hand thrusting towards her. It was clenched, but—as it did not appear to be holding anything—she decided that the intention was to catch her by the shoulder, or knock her down with a blow. Instinctively and without any conscious guidance, the Webley R.I.C. revolver lifted and she squeezed the trigger, which required only a light pressure with the action cocked. Nor, at such close quarters, was there any need for her to take aim. Yet, in spite of delivering a Boxer cartridge's[1] .422 calibre bullet to the centre of her assailant's chest, which elicited a squeal that was feminine in its timbre, she had not reacted quite swiftly enough. Even as the figure was jolted away from her, she felt something thin and sharp being thrust into the left side of her throat. Whatever it was sank deeply before being withdrawn as its wielder tumbled backwards.

Inside the building, for all the difficulty involved when using even a short barrelled revolver in such a manner, the bearded anarchist came very close to achieving his purpose. As the muzzle blast from the detonated black powder was

1. "Boxer" cartridge: an early form of self-contained metal centre-fire bullet designed by an Englishman, Colonel Boxer, primarily for use by the British armed forces. Comprised of a thin coiled brass case with an iron base-head and separate cap chamber, it was relatively effective and cheap to manufacture, but was rendered obsolete when the sturdier drawn brass cases were produced commercially.—*J.T.E.*

igniting his pocket, the expelled bullet flew to rip off Dusty's hat.

The small Texan did not allow himself to be deterred or distracted by his narrow escape. While relieving himself of the second man, his left hand was already crossing to the right side Colt. Being aware of the problems involved when discharging a firearm as "Gotz" had done, he saw no reason to change his intentions. At that moment, the man with the injured foot was the most immediate danger. He was already liberating his weapon and was under no restrictions as to how he could use it. Flowing from its holster, Dusty's bone-handled Colt was turned, lined and fired in a blur of movement. While it, too, was aimed by instinctive alignment, its owner had no cause for complaint over the result.

Looking around as the bullet struck the man between the eyes and killed him instantly, Dusty noticed in passing that "Gotz" was being compelled to withdraw his hand from the burning pocket. Then his gaze went to the last of the anarchists, who had been brought to a halt by colliding with the wall. He too was far from out of action and demonstrated an ability as a gun-handler on a par with that of his now dead companion. So it was obvious to the small Texan that he must be dealt with before any further attention could be devoted to his leader.

At that moment, something observed out of the corner of his eye warned Dusty that his position was becoming even more desperate. Despite the flames, "Gotz" had not released the Storekeeper and was bringing it clear of the pocket.

There would not be time to cope with both men!

Frightened by what had happened, the maid ran past the writhing figure that was sprawling on the ground and wondered disinterestedly who it might be, but had no intention of stopping to find out. Apart from the initial stab of pain and a smarting where the point had entered and had been pulled out, she felt nothing and doubted that she was seriously hurt. Then a sensation of tightening began to affect her muscles and agony of a numbing, soul-searing kind impinged itself upon her whole being. She staggered, stumbled and tried to scream, but no sound came. With legs buckling beneath her, she measured her length on the ground to twitch and jerk away what remained of her life.[2]

Kicked open by Waco, the door burst inwards with such force that its rotten wood was torn from the hinges. Showing the co-ordination acquired while working as Dusty's deputies in Mulrooney, Kansas, he and the Kid plunged into the room practically simultaneously. Having been anticipating trouble, or the possibility of it, they were following their training as peace officers by carrying offensive rather than defensive weapons. A glance was all they needed to inform them how they might best use the rifles they carried to their *amigo's* benefit.

Held at waist level spurts of flame began to erupt from the Winchester Model of 1866 rifle as the black dressed Texan operated its lever and worked the trigger with great rapidity. Engulfed in a veritable torrent of flying lead, the bare-footed man was briefly held against the wall by five of the ten bullets sent in his direction.

Snapping the butt of the rifle to his shoulder, Waco took the instant needed to aim and fired. His bullet ploughed into "Gotz's" right shoulder while the Storekeeper was still lifting towards Dusty. Spun around and dropping his gun, the anarchist tried to run away. Before he reached the door through which the maid had departed, the small Texan tackled him around the legs. Brought down hard enough to drive all the air from his lungs, although the landing put out the fire in his pocket, he was in no condition to struggle even if the muzzle of Dusty's Colt had not been pressed against the side of his head.

"Get out back and grab the woman!" the small Texan yelled. "Watch her. She's armed."

"Yo!" replied the Kid, using the traditional cavalry acknowledgement of an order.

2. While working on the manuscript, the author has discovered that *curare* relaxes the "end plates" between the nerves and muscles, preventing the heart and lungs functioning thereby causing death by asphyxiation. So he assumes some form of strychnine—most varieties of which produce convulsions and stiffening of the muscles—was the basis of Beguinage's poison.—*J.T.E.*

"Sit up!" Dusty commanded, rising as the black clad Texan ran from the room.

Several seconds elapsed before "Gotz" could obey. From outside came a startled exclamation, followed by the glow of a match ignited by the Kid.

"D-Don't kill me!" the anarchist gasped, shuffling until his back was against the wall and staring at the two young Texans.

"Why shouldn't we?" Waco demanded, working his Winchester's lever and pointing its muzzle at the bearded, frightened face. "You was planning to do it to Dusty."

"L-Let me live and I'll tell you where to find the woman if she gets away," "Gotz" offered.

"You're a mite too late for that, *hombre*," the Kid announced returning. "She's out there, dead and, unless I'm mistook, so's Beguinage's woman."

CHAPTER THIRTEEN

Hunting Can Be Dangerous

"How did it go, Miss Amelia?" Florence Drakefield inquired, watching the beautiful Englishwoman slipping into a night-gown.

"I wish I knew," Amelia Benkinsop admitted, sitting on the bed.

The reception had been terminated shortly after Dusty Fog's departure. Crown Prince Rudolph of Bosgravnia had suggested that he was tired and taking the hint Senator and Mrs. Blaby had set about dispersing the guests so that he could retire. The Lady had not been sorry to make her way to the room which had been allocated to her, and the maid had arrived to attend to her needs. While the latter was unnecessary, she had welcomed the opportunity to discuss the happenings of the evening.

"Why did you ask Captain Fog to go outside with you?" the maid inquired, puzzled by her mistress's air of perturbation.

"I didn't," Amelia corrected. "He told me we'd go."

"He'd a nerve!" Florence snorted indignantly, although she knew the blonde was not the kind to accept orders mildly from strangers.

"Not necessarily," Amelia replied. "It was just that he knows I'm *not* Freddie Besgrove-Woodstole."

"Heh?" Florence gasped.

"Of all the infernal luck, Freddie owns a saloon in Mulrooney, Kansas, wherever that might be," the Lady elaborated, with just a suggestion of bitterness. "And, unless I'm sadly mistaken, she and Captain Fog are on *very* good terms."

"Oooer!" the maid breathed, realizing the implications of what she had just been told. "Shall we take stoppo?"

"It's too late for *that*," Amelia smiled, knowing the word

"stoppo" meant to run away in the argot of London's criminal element. "Anyway, it isn't necessary and wouldn't be polite. We're invited to be guests on the royal hunt."

"I *knew* you'd get him to ask you," Florence declared, having been aware that the blonde had hoped to obtain permission and never doubting she would be successful.

"On the contrary," Amelia answered, "I don't think Rudolph knew that dear Charlene and I would be accompanying him."

"*Charlene*—!" the maid repeated and the one word was indicative of a far from favourable or respectful regard for the *Comtesse de* Petain. "When did he ask *her*?"

"To be precise, my dear, he *didn't*," the Lady replied. "I could be wrong, but I doubt whether he had even thought about inviting either of us when Captain Fog told us in the garden that we were going."

"But—?" Florence yelped.

"I know exactly what you mean," Amelia sighed, running fingers through her hair in a gesture redolent of mystification. "My acquaintance with Captain Fog hasn't been extensive, but I'm sure he's not the kind of person who would forget *anything* important. Yet when he told the *Comtesse* that I had been invited, he also said he had forgotten to mention she was invited too. What is he up to?"

"Don't ask me," Florence requested, starting to gather her mistress's clothes.

"Why does he want us to go with them?" Amelia went on, speaking half to herself. "Is it because he believes my story, or so that he can keep his eye on both of us?"

"What do *you* think?" the maid inquired, her attitude suggesting complete confidence in the blonde's ability to produce the correct solution.

"That I wish I had your faith in me, for one thing," Amelia smiled, then became serious. "I would like to think it's because he trusts me and wants me to watch her. But, whatever the reason, I have the feeling that dear Charlene isn't terribly taken with the idea of having the pleasure of my company."

"Cheeky cow!" Florence snorted, resenting the possibility of her well-respected employer being slighted by what, in her insular British fashion, she regarded as a not too savoury foreigner. "She deserves a maid like she's got."

"Speaking of the maid, I don't remember seeing much of her towards the end of the reception."

"That's because she wasn't there."

"Where did she go?"

"To our room, with a headache she said. But she wasn't there when the butler sent me to look for her."

"What time was this?"

"When Mrs. Blaby started getting the guests ready to go home."

"Perhaps she's gone to the *Comtesse's* room," Amelia suggested.

"Not her," Florence declared. "I looked after I'd made sure she didn't know how to pick a lock and get in here."

"It's probably not important where she went," the Lady decided, knowing full well that her own maid had the skill to pick a lock and deducing that it had been put to use. "Most likely she has a gentleman friend she wanted to see."

"Any bloke who'd go out with the likes of her must want it bad," Florence stated. "Stuck up, snobbish cow she is."

"You don't appear to like her," Amelia remarked.

"No more than you like her boss," the maid admitted. "What'd she have to say about you going on the hunt?"

"She pointed out how terribly strenuous, uncomfortable and unpleasantly primitive it would be," the Lady replied pensively. "And how she didn't think someone as delicately raised as I would be able to stand its rigours."

"*You*?" Florence gasped, as if hardly able to believe her ears. "How about *her* in that case?"

"Oh she'll be all right," Amelia answered dryly. "But she says that she wouldn't consider going if she didn't carry out a programme of exercises every day to keep her in tip-top physical condition."

"That's certainly true," Florence affirmed, having completed the task of putting away her mistress's clothing while they were talking. "The girls downstairs told me she asked Mrs. Blaby if she could use the empty stable at the back of the house, and she goes there every morning. Everybody's been told to keep away while she's in it."

"Hum!" Amelia said, standing up and stretching. "Then I hope she's told Mrs. Blaby I've been invited to join her tomorrow morning."

"Why?" the maid demanded suspiciously.

"Probably so that she can prove to me how unsuited I am for the rigours of the hunt," the Lady guessed. "It was more of a challenge than an invitation."

"You don't think she's going to make sure you can't go on the hunt?" Florence asked.

"I don't think she would try anything so drastic," Amelia replied, having considered the possibility.

"I wouldn't put it past her if she thought she could get away with it," Florence stated. "And she's up to *something*, anyway."

"Well, there's only one way to find out what it is," the Lady declared, glancing at her open trunk. "Let's see if we can find anything appropriate for me to wear when I go to do it."

"Good morning, Lady Winifred," Charlene greeted, a suggestion of mockery in her voice. "I wondered if you would come and join me."

"I said I would," Amelia answered, her air of defiance combining with a suggestion of apprehension, as she studied the other woman's appearance.

Although the *Comtesse* had been informed of her maid's death before leaving her room at the mansion, she showed neither regret nor remorse. On hearing the news, her only emotions were anger over the realization that she had been tricked and relief at learning the woman was not taken alive to divulge whatever information might have been obtained regarding her faction's plans for the assassination of the Crown Prince.

Originally built to house the small ponies suitable for use by the Blabys' now grown-up and departed children, the stable in which the Lady had joined the *Comtesse* was not large enough to fill the needs of saddle- or carriage horses. So, although the stalls had not been removed, it now served as a store for forage. Otherwise unoccupied, it held bales of hay, sacks of grain and the implements necessary to handle them.

Standing with her right hand and left foot resting on the top of the centre stall's gate, like a dancer using a wall bar in training, the play of firm arm and leg muscles proved Charlene's adherence to a rigorous programme of exercises was beneficial. Nor was it any wonder that, while making her way from her room to the stable, she had worn the long black cloak which was now hanging on the gate. A white silk band held back her brunette tresses. She had on a sleeveless black leotard and matching tights that fitted like a second skin and showed there were no other garments beneath them. Thin black leather riding gloves covered her hands and ballet-shoes graced her feet. The whole effect of the ensemble was sensual in the extreme, but also a little sinister when considered in conjunction with the expression of her beautiful features.

As at the previous night's reception, Amelia's attire was far less revealing and she had had no need to cover it for the walk to the stable. The neck of her plain white blouse was unbuttoned, but it was not open to an indecorous length. For all that, it was sufficiently tight to show she was as well endowed physically as the *Comtesse*. Equally unostentatious, her black skirt was just long enough to show she was wearing a pair of bedroom slippers. Mindful of Charlene's remarks when suggesting she joined in the exercises, she too was wearing black riding gloves to avoid soiling her hands.

"You should try this kind of exercise," the *Comtesse* remarked, raising and swinging her left leg up and down effortlessly in the fashion of a dancer. "Although you would find it far too strenuous."

"I used to do it at school," Amelia protested mildly.

"And stopped as soon as you left," Charlene guessed, and walked forward, performing a couple of graceful pirouettes, while continuing, "You know, my dear, I really don't think you should accept Rudy's invitation."

"Why shouldn't I?" the Lady asked, putting her hands on her hips in a gesture of petulant indignation.

"Hunting can be dangerous," Charlene explained, sounding solicitous and confident that she was correct in her assessment of the Englishwoman being a pampered milksop who could easily be frightened into accepting her wishes. Measuring the distance between them as she commenced what appeared to be another pirouette, she went on, "All kinds of accidents can happen. Like *this*!"

Simultaneously with uttering the last two words, the *Comtesse* snapped her right leg sideways in a horizontal circular motion. Its purpose was that of the French style of foot-boxing called *savate* rather than part of a ballet training exercise. However, if she had been less assured that her motive for inviting the blonde to the stable had not been suspected, she might have noticed that her action was not entirely unexpected.

In spite of anticipating something of the sort when she saw Charlene's footwear, the speed and precision of the attack still took Amelia almost unawares. She had left moving away and trying to grab the rapidly approaching limb an instant too late. Passing between her hands before they could catch hold and deflect it, the foot reached her stomach. Contact was made with somewhat less force than had been intended, but nevertheless it was sufficiently hard to hurt her. Croaking in pain and folding at the waist, she stumbled back a few steps to trip and collapse on to her hands and knees. Looking up while sucking in air to replenish her depleted lungs, she saw her assailant walking towards her like a cat stalking a mouse.

"So tell him!—that you have!—changed your mind!" Charlene ordered, punctuating each third word by driving the hard-packed toe of her left ballet shoe against the Lady's ribs. Ensuing gasps from Amelia proved they were being felt. Then she bent to sink her right hand into the blonde's back hair, grasped the waistband of the skirt with her left and began to lift, exclaiming, "Do you hear, you Engli—?"

The question was terminated by a startled and anguished squawk much like those Amelia had been emitting when kicked and for a similar reason. Instead of begging for mercy, or struggling in a feebly ineffectual fashion—the only contingencies envisaged by the *Comtesse*—the Lady produced a far more positive repayment for the punishment inflicted upon her. She was unable to prevent herself from being hauled upwards in a painful manner, but did not wait until she was fully erect before responding. Thrusting her bent left arm to the rear with all the force she could muster, she rammed its elbow into Charlene's *solar plexus*.

As with the first kick Amelia had taken, the jab she delivered failed to achieve its maximum effect. The effort being exerted by the *Comtesse* to lift her victim had caused her stomach muscles to tense. Although she released the Lady, bent over with hands clutching at the stricken region and staggered backwards, she suffered far less than would have been the case if she had been relaxed when the blow landed.

"How right you are, *Comtesse*," Amelia purred, straightening up and, doubting whether the affair was over, starting to unfasten her skirt. "Accidents *do* happen—and not only when one is on a hunt."

In one respect, Charlene had been more fortunate than the Lady. She came to a halt without falling down. Watching what was happening, she began to suspect that her judgement might have been at fault once again. When she had lured the Englishwoman to the stable, she had believed she would be dealing with a pampered, soft-living victim who could be terrified into refusing the invitation and keeping quiet about why she had changed her mind. From the way the other had reacted since she launched the attack, it seemed that her summation was wrong.

The *Comtesse's* revised point of view received further confirmation as Amelia's skirt began to slide down. Instead of the decorous underwear that she had expected to be revealed, the blonde was wearing black tights similar to her own. Such a revelation came as a surprise and aroused disturbing speculations. It implied that her reason for arranging the meeting had been suspected. Therefore the Englishwoman had *not* walked into her trap, but had arrived anticipating some such eventuality. What was more, Charlene's instincts as she rubbed gingerly at the spot where the blow had landed warned that she could be up against a formidable antagonist.

The kind of fury that she had only just managed to control at the Portside Hotel when Alex von Farlenheim had taunted her over the error she had made by hiring "*Rapido*" Clint" boiled through the *Comtesse*. It drove all thought of the possible consequences from her. Letting out a shriek of profanity in her native tongue, she darted forward to try and come to grips before Amelia obtained the extra freedom of movement that the removal of the skirt would permit.

Appreciating what was intended, the Lady found herself unable to avert it. She had hoped to step out of the skirt, but it had only descended as far as her ankles when the *Comtesse* reached her. Raising her left leg out of the garment was the best she could accomplish. So she twisted her torso and snapped a punch with her right fist in an attempt to fend off hands which were thrusting in her direction. Her knuckles dug into the thinly covered mound of Charlene's left breast, but achieved no more than producing a squeak of pain. Then the brunette's right fingers sank into her hair, pulling at it hard, while the other arm encircled her waist.

Caught with only one foot on the floor, the impetus of her attacker's arrival threw Amelia off balance. Digging her own hands into the brunette tresses as well as the head band would allow, by instinct rather than conscious intention, she contrived to drag the *Comtesse* down with her in such a manner that they alighted side by side. In spite of having learned more effective methods, as had been evident in the opening exchanges, they continued to fight in a purely feminine fashion once they landed.

Over and over the embattled pair rolled, struggling, with the same thought in each head. Realizing the advantage it offered, neither was willing to let the other gain the upper position if she could help it. Being so evenly matched in height, weight and determination, it was impossible for either to remain on top more than briefly when she got there. Their writhing bodies ground together as they went back and forward across the stable floor. Hands tore at hair, slapped, punched, clutched, plucked and pulled at clothing indiscriminately. Entwined legs flailed, kicked, kneed and thrust in an equally random fashion. All the time, the air reverberated with the sound of slaps, the crisper thuds of punches, tearing cloth, squeals, gasps, squeaks and profane exclamations as garments were torn or blows landed on faces, shoulders, backs and breasts.

Gasping for breath and almost at a stalemate, crashing into a wall caused the women to roll apart and come to their knees. Each had a knee burst through her tights. Amelia had lost her blouse and bodice and the *Comtesse's* leotard had been dragged from her shoulders, leaving them both naked to the waist. Paying not the slightest attention to their condition of semi-nudity and oblivious of the blood running from their nostrils, they began to swing at each other with flat hands or clenched fists. Then, almost as if they had reached a mutual decision, they brought the exchange to an end. Lunging together, they threw their arms around one another. Locked in a bosom to bosom clinch, they struggled to their feet.

After staggering in a circle with hands scrabbling and legs delivering kicks which missed as often as they landed, a push from Amelia sent Charlene reeling across the stable. Brought to a halt by hitting the gate of a stall, the *Comtesse* noticed a pitchfork sticking from a nearby bale of hay. A glance told her that the blonde was following to continue the attack and, croaking almost breathless obscenities in French, she flung herself sideways to pluck it free.

Throwing herself at a greater speed across the intervening distance, Amelia also grabbed the pitchfork before it could be turned upon her. Then she and Charlene each tried to wrest it from the other's grasp. Surging a few steps in first one, then another direction, perspiration flowed more freely as they exerted all their strength to their efforts. At first, it seemed that they were once more at a stalemate. Then the *Comtesse* sensed that she was weakening. Feeling the other's legs buckle a little, the Lady called upon a rapidly flagging reserve of energy and expended it in a twisting heave.

Letting out a moaning wail of distress, Charlene lost her hold on the pitchfork and was sent sprawling to fall face down near the stable door. She rolled exhaustedly on to her back, but was capable of no more. Supine and spent after the exertions of the fight, tears of defeat blurred her vision. Vaguely she saw the Englishwoman approaching. In spite of staggering and looking almost ready to collapse, the dishevelled and badly fatigued blonde came to a halt with her feet straddling her victim. She swung the pitchfork up, its gleaming tines pointing at Charlene's heaving, exposed bosom and the Frenchwoman knew there was nothing she could do to prevent it from being driven home.

Having heard that Amelia had been seen going to the stable where Charlene was in the habit of taking her morning exercises, Dusty Fog had decided to disregard Mrs. Blaby's instructions that it should be considered off limits while the *Comtesse* was using it. He believed that he was justified in going against his hostess's wishes under the circumstances. The deaths of Charlene's maid and Beguinage's female accomplice, along with the arrest of the wounded "Gotz" and the local anarchist, had not ended the threat to Crown Prince Rudolph of Bosgravnia's life. Nor did Alex von Farlenheim being sent away in disgrace rule out the possibility of danger from the aristocratic faction.

In spite of having been impressed by the sincerity with which the Lady had stated she wanted to prevent harm befalling the royal visitor, the small Texan had not ruled out the possibility that it was merely well simulated. Whether real or false, he was curious about her private meeting with the *Comtesse*. There had been a very marked lack of cordiality between them the previous evening, but that too could have been no more than acting their parts in a conspiracy.

Before Dusty arrived at the stable, he saw and heard enough to consider it was unlikely that Amelia and Charlene had met for a friendly, or mutually advantageous discussion. Not only were there sounds suggestive of women engaged in physical conflict, but the behaviour of the Lady's maid gave strength to the assumption. Looking in the window, she was acting in a manner reminiscent of a spectator at a prize fight. Although she did not shout encouragement, she ducked, bobbed her head and made punching motions with her fists. At the same time, her face expressed delight or sympathy depending upon how her employer was faring.

"What's going on?" Dusty demanded.

"Oh, it's you, Captain Fog!" Florence said, after giving a start of alarm and swinging around. She stood with her back to the window, trying to prevent him from seeing what was happening inside. "Lady Winifred and the *Comtesse* are just taking their morning exercises."

Neither the excuse nor the attempt to block the small Texan's view was successful. What he saw over the maid's shoulder informed him that nothing so innocuous was taking place. Also that there was an urgent need for outside intervention. Swinging around, he ran towards the door and hoped he would be in time to save the *Comtesse* from being killed.

On the point of driving the pitchfork into her recumbent and all but helpless foe, sense returned to Amelia. She realized that to have fought could be excused, as Charlene had been the aggressor, the same would not apply if she terminated it in such a manner. Flinging the device aside, she sank to kneel astride the *Comtesse's* torso. Even as she delivered a punch to the jaw which knocked Charlene out, the door burst open.

"H-Hello, Captain Fog," Amelia gasped, staring at the small Texan as he sprang into the stable. "Th-The *Comtesse* told me I couldn't stand the rigours of the hunt. But I think she may have changed her mind."

CHAPTER FOURTEEN

You're Still *Alive*

"DON'T you think that it is time for us to go back to the camp?" Captain Fritz von Farlenheim inquired, glancing upwards through the foliage of the woodland at the darkening sky. "It is getting late and Uncle Ludwig has arranged for that conjurer to entertain us this evening."

"Let me see if I can collect another rabbit or two, or at least another bird, in that clearing," requested Charlene, *Comtesse de* Petain, gesturing to an opening among the trees ahead of them with the shotgun she was carrying. "I do so want to take back a better bag than Lady Winifred collected yesterday, Fritz, and just a couple more will beat her."

Ten days had elapsed since the disastrous confrontation Charlene had brought about between herself and the beautiful blonde Englishwoman she still believed to be Lady Winifred Amelia Besgrove Woodstole. In spite of her belated regrets over having provoked the incident, she considered that everything was still progressing in a satisfactory manner and the culmination of her plan to assassinate Crown Prince Rudolph of Bosgravnia was approaching its climax.

Travelling almost due west from Corpus Christie, the royal visitor's hunting expedition had set up its first base camp in Duval County about five miles north of the town of San Diego. To avoid being requested to attend official receptions, or receiving visits from the citizens, they had not informed the local authorities of their presence. However, while their privacy in that respect had been attained, Ludwig von Farlenheim had obtained the services of a well known medicine showman to give a performance on the second evening after their arrival. Charlene knew why this had been arranged, but was unaware of much else that had happened recently.

Dusty Fog had co-operated with Sheriff Elvis Tragg in

dealing with "Gotz" and the local anarchist. Interrogating them, the peace officer and the small Texan had been satisfied that their faction could now be discounted as a threat to the Crown Prince's well-being. Finding themselves in the hands of the law, they had been so eager to save their skins that each had supplied sufficient information to convince their captors there was nothing more to fear from their associates. Unfortunately, neither could produce any evidence to incriminate Charlene. Although the dead maid had learned that a party of aristocrats also hoped to assassinate the royal visitor, and knew of "*Rapido* Clint's" true identity, she either had not known, or did not take the men into her confidence, about any plans that had been made to kill Rudolph.

Having failed to acquire any evidence against the *Comtesse*, Dusty had decided to let her accompany the expedition so that a watch could be kept upon her. It had been as a result of Amelia Benkinsop's quick wits that this had been brought about. Questioned about the fight by an indignant Mrs. Blaby —who had considered such unladylike behaviour should preclude either participant from accompanying the royal visitor—in the presence of the small Texan, Governor Stanton Howard and Liebenfrau, she had claimed that catch-as-catch-can wrestling had become all the rage as a sport—albeit in private—among female members of the European aristocracy. Finding that she and the *Comtesse* had a mutual interest, they had met for a friendly bout. Because of inadequate supervision and the lack of proper facilities, it had degenerated into a situation for which they were both ashamed and deeply contrite. Inadvertently putting too much gusto into their efforts, they had hurt one another and lost their tempers. However, they were now sorry for what had happened and neither bore any ill will. In proof of this, as Charlene had lost her maid, the Lady had already offered to share Florence Drakefield's services with her on the hunting trip. Seeing that the only hope of being able to carry out her plan lay in agreeing, much as having to do so and conceding that she had been well and truly beaten by the Englishwoman rankled, the *Comtesse* had supported Amelia's story. She had drawn comfort from the thought that her honour would be avenged when the scheme was brought to fruition.

Hampered by his lack of trained assistants, Tragg had done all he could to learn about the woman who had met her end while killing Charlene's maid. Medical evidence had determined that she had used the same means as had murdered the town marshal and Liebenfrau's orderly. She had also been identified as the saloongirl who had befriended the three men involved in the first attempt to gun down "*Rapido* Clint," but neither the sheriff nor Buck Raffles were able to connect her with the second pair. What was more, her attire on the night she had died had been more suitable to a moderately affluent "good" woman than an employee of a cheap saloon, and none of the garments had been purchased in the United States. In spite of it being unlikely that she had acquired a private residence since arriving in Corpus Christie, no hotel or rooming house had reported she was missing. Nor had a request for information, accompanied by an illustration of her features, in the local newspaper produced results before the expedition had taken its departure. Tragg had had no greater success in discovering where Beguinage or "Gustav Breakast" had been staying in the town, but had promised to notify Dusty if he should do so.

There had only been one major incident before the party set off. A lengthy telegraph message had informed Ludwig von Farlenheim that his younger nephew had met with a fatal accident during the voyage to Brownsville. According to the captain of the ship, who had sent the news, Alex had started to drink heavily as soon as they left port. Walking alone on the open deck after dark on the second night, he had been seen to lose his balance as the vessel rolled and he had tumbled over the rail. Although the ship had been put about and a search made, he was not found. Nor, in the captain's opinion, could he have survived to reach the shore alive with such a high sea running, even if he had been sober. Von Farlenheim had admitted to feeling at least partially to blame for his nephew's death, but he had not allowed grief to interfere with his efforts to make the royal visitor's hunting trip a success.

While the expedition was neither as large nor luxurious as

some which had been organized for other visiting members of the European nobility,[1] it was well equipped and comfortable. Until Amelia and Charlene had recovered from the effects of the fight, they had ridden with Florence in a *Britschka*[2] carriage imported from England by Ludwig von Farlenheim. Designed for long distance travel over poor or non-existent roads, they had sufficient room to sleep in it at night and there was adequate storage for their baggage. Two large wagons transported the men's belongings, four good-sized wall tents, equipment and supplies, including a selection of drinks and enough food to supplement the meat acquired once hunting had been commenced. The vehicles had been driven by the Bosgravnian orderlies, one of whom was also an excellent cook.

Noticing how the *Comtesse* had sought to ingratiate herself with the, Crown Prince and his retinue since leaving Corpus Christie, Dusty had wondered if she was cutting her losses by giving up her support of the aristocratic faction and hoping to gain Rudolph's favour. Having no wish to confirm that he was still suspicious of her, the small Texan had decided against trying to get her to betray her former associates. So far, only the Crown Prince, Liebenfrau and his three *amigos* were aware of her connection with them and he wanted it kept that way. Subjected to an equally careful surveillance, Amelia had done nothing to suggest that she had been lying when explaining why she had come to the United States.

Compelled to travel in the same vehicle until they were in a condition to ride on horseback had been something of a strain for the Lady and Charlene, but they had managed to maintain nothing worse than an icily polite attitude towards one another. The only noticeable evidence of their continued antipathy had manifested itself in their obvious rivalry. No matter

1. In 1854, an Englishman, Sir George Gore, hired the famous mountain man, Jim Bridger, as his guide and had a retinue of around fifty men. During 1871–72, Grand Duke Alexis hunted with an escort headed by Generals Philip H. Sheridan and George Armstrong Custer, with William F. (Buffalo Bill) Cody as his chief guide.—*J.T.E.*
2. The *Britschka* originated in Poland and was introduced into Britain in the early 1820's, finding favour because of its carrying capacity and comfort.—*J.T.E.*

what one did, the other would invariably try to better. Each
had requested a mount as an alternative to being carried in the
Britschka before she had really felt up to sitting a saddle because the other had done so. In addition to displaying their
respective equestrian skill, another area of contention had
arisen from mutual ability to handle a shotgun. Finding that
they both possessed considerable proficiency, they had offered
to keep the party supplied with small game for the pot, thus
allowing the men to concentrate upon collecting more worthwhile trophies.

The difficulty of hunting while on the move all day had
tended to restrict competition between the women during the
journey, but once they had arrived at the first base camp the
rivalry blossomed. Having been less successful than Amelia
the previous day, none of the party had been surprised when
Charlene had expressed her determination to go out again and
improve on her performance. It had been decided that, being
new to Texas, neither of the women would hunt alone. So
Charlene had asked Fritz von Farlenheim to accompany her.
She had also suggested that, although it had proved comparatively unproductive when she had been there with his uncle as
her escort the day before, they should visit the woodland
about two miles west of the camp. They had arrived there in
the early afternoon, finding some game; but not quite enough
to satisfy her.

Wishing to avoid attracting any more attention than was
necessary, the members of the Crown Prince's retinue did not
wear their uniforms. Instead, they were clad in clothing purchased at Corpus Christie. While there, Rudolph and Fritz had
also acquired Western-style gunbelts with open-topped holsters. However, there had been more than just an outwards
change where the First Taster was concerned. Impressed by
the four young Texans' competence, he had lost his attitude of
superiority towards them. In fact, he had followed his leader's
example and treated them as social equals. He had unbent to
such an extent that he had not become annoyed when his
choice of a British Adams .450 revolver was subjected to criti-
cism by Waco during a debate about the relative merits of
various types of firearms around the campfire one night.

Fritz was dressed in the style of a working cowhand and

had the Adams hanging in its holster on his right hip. As a precaution in case they should come across some animal that was too large to be dealt with by Charlene's shotgun, he was carrying a Winchester Model of 1873 carbine.

For her part, the *Comtesse* had on a two piece travelling costume. Its jacket was open and, attached to the left side of her leather waistbelt was a cross-draw holster in which rode the short-barrelled Webley Royal Irish Constabulary revolver her maid had appropriated on the night the anarchist faction was wiped out. She had purchased the rig shortly after her arrival at Brownsville, claiming that she had heard so many frightful stories about Texas that she felt it was advisable for her to go armed when travelling. Amelia had taken a similar precaution and a competition between them had established that they were both competent shots with a handgun.

Scanning the terrain ahead as he and Charlene emerged from the trees and advanced across the small clearing, Fritz failed to notice that she was not carrying the shotgun in a manner conducive to being brought into action quickly if some kind of quarry was present. Instead, she had the barrels resting on her left shoulder and was gripping the wrist of the butt with her right hand. Furthermore, not only did she allow him to take the lead, she moved until she was walking directly behind him and would be unable to shoot without endangering his life. Not that there appeared to be any need for a posture of greater readiness on her part. The clearing was devoid of animals and birds.

"Bad luck, Charlene," Fritz commiserated. "There's nothing here."

"I thought I saw a rabbit or something moving under the bushes between those two big trees over there," the *Comtesse* replied, without taking the shotgun from her shoulder. "Let's take a look and, if we don't find anything, we'll go back to camp."

In spite of her suggestion, Charlene made no attempt to take a more advantageous position or remedy her state of unpreparedness as she followed her escort. Devoting his attention to searching beneath the bush she had mentioned, he had almost reached it before he found out that they were not the only human beings in the vicinity. Three men stepped from behind the trees. All wore range clothes, with low-tied Colt revolvers, but he had eyes for only one of them.

"Alex!" Fritz gasped, too amazed to do anything other than halt and stare at his supposedly drowned cousin. "You're still *alive*!"

"You don't seem any too pleased about it," Alex von Farlenheim replied, also employing their native tongue. "But then, you never were. And this is another time you won't have cause to be."

"But—!" Fritz croaked, then he realized that there must be some sinister reason for the false report of his cousin's death, and his right hand went with some speed to the butt of the Adams revolver.

Instead of duplicating his action, although the men with Alex were competent to have done so, the three newcomers sprang towards the First Taster. Being aware that he had acquired a reasonable skill at making a fast draw under the Texans' tutelage, Charlene was disinclined to take chances. As soon as the trio appeared, she had begun to lift the shotgun from her shoulder. Catching the barrels deftly in her left hand, she propelled the butt around horizontally. Passing beneath the wide brim of Fritz's hat, it crashed against the base of his skull. Going down, with bright lights seeming to be bursting inside his head, he heard her shouting for the men to catch him so that his clothing would not be made dirty. Then, as he felt hands grabbing him and preventing him from reaching the ground, he became unconscious.

"Help Mr. von Farlenheim to change clothes with him," Charlene commanded, as the men supported their limp burden.

"Sure thing," replied the taller of Alex's companions, eyeing the *Comtesse* in a way that showed he resented being given an order by her. "Shall we do it *here*, so's you can watch we do it right?"

"I will wait at the other side of the clearing," Charlene answered, bristling with indignation at such disrespect from a man she knew to be a hired killer and whom she regarded as a far from savoury, if necessary, employee. "Hurry—*please*!"

"Yes—*ma'am*," the resentful man growled, the pause indicating that the use of the honorific was meant to sound as much of an after-thought as the *Comtesse's* last word had been. "Do you-all have any special way you want him killed when we're—"

"Cut it out!" growled the slightly shorter of the hired guns. "Time's wasting and we don't want *anybody*, especially the Ysabel Kid, coming looking for them."

"I've told them to leave Fritz alive until it's over," Alex informed Charlene, as he joined her about fifteen minutes later. He was now wearing his cousin's clothing, but—although it was now too dark for her to notice—had retained his own gunbelt and revolver.

"Why?" Charlene demanded.

"So I can tell him that it was because of him the noble Rudolph was done to death," Alex explained, his face aglow with savage satisfaction. "When he hears how, we won't have to kill him. He'll be so mortified that he'll do it himself."

CHAPTER FIFTEEN

If I'm Wrong, I'll Get Hell

"COME on, Fritz!" Crown Prince Rudolph of Bosgravnia called with cheerful impatience, looking at the man he assumed to be his First Taster who was just jumping down from the wagon in which the food and intoxicating liquors were stored. "If you must do your duty, hurry along with it. You're keeping the good Doctor waiting."

"Yes, Fritz, get a move on," seconded Charlene, *Comtesse de* Petain. "I've heard so much about Doctor Seraphin that I can't wait to see him perform."

Sitting next to Ludwig von Farlenheim at the right end of the long and sturdy collapsible table that was one of the facilities he had provided for the hunting party's comfort—and with a more sinister purpose in mind—Charlene was eagerly awaiting more than the commencement of the entertainment. The scheme which she had hatched with him was approaching its culmination. Looking around, a sense of contentment and fulfilment welled through her. In spite of the various contretemps and mishaps that had threatened to ruin her endeavours, she was confident that at last everything was going as had been planned.

Having been compelled to leave Bosgravnia in disgrace, von Farlenheim had blamed the ruling family for his downfall. Nor had being well provided for and becoming a successful business man in the New World lessened his hatred. Learning of the Council of Noble Birth's intention, from a cousin who had visited him, he had offered his services. When told what would be required of him, he had stated that—although he possessed the necessary contacts locally—he felt it was advisable to employ an outside agency rather than somebody from his home town.

The precaution had proved justified when, without consult-

ing von Farlenheim, Governor Stanton Howard had arranged
for Ole Devil Hardin's floating outfit to act as the royal visitor's escort. Fortunately, "Gustav Breakast's" local second-in-
command had been poisoned by Beguinage before Dusty Fog
reached him and the go-between's death at the hands of Town
Marshal Benjamin Digbry had prevented him from being captured and interrogated by the small Texan. Prior to them having met their ends, they had arranged for all the specialized
help that was needed to implement the scheme.

Taken all in all, Charlene considered that the intervention
of Europe's "premier assassin" had been more beneficial than
detrimental to her cause. While he had warned her against
trying to kill the Crown Prince, he had refrained from taking
measures that would ensure she could not. His own death and
that of his female accomplice had removed any further threat
to her from that direction. What was more, the woman had
disposed of a much closer source of danger. If the treacherous
maid had been arrested with the other anarchists, she would
undoubtedly have disclosed anything she had learned in an
attempt to save her own skin.

From that point, except for the *Comtesse*'s error in judgement where the character of "Lady Winifred Amelia Besgrove-Woodstole" was concerned, everything had flowed
along smoothly. She was drawing considerable satisfaction
from the thought that her defeat at the Englishwoman's hands
would soon be avenged in no uncertain manner.

By provoking the quarrel with his cousin and letting there
be no doubt he was the aggressor, Alex von Farlenheim had
provided an excuse for having himself sent away. His "disgrace" had also offered an acceptable reason for what was to
come next. Without being aware of the coincidence, he had
been put ashore and met at the point selected by the Ysabel
Kid for the rendezvous with the U.S.S. *Nantucket*. As Amelia
Benkinsop had guessed, it was an area known to smugglers,
and the captain of the ship had once been in that line of work.
On reaching Brownsville, he had completed the work he was
hired to perform by sending the telegraph message to inform
Ludwig of his younger nephew's "accidental death." While
this was happening, Alex had accompanied the men he had
met to the vicinity of the hunting party's first base camp.

Because of the necessity for the Crown Prince's whereabouts
to be known at all times, in case news of importance had to be
passed to him, it had not been possible for his itinerary to be
kept a complete secret and Ludwig had known their destination.

The basic scheme had been evolved before the involvement
of Ole Devil's floating outfit, but their presence had caused a
few minor changes. Not only had the hired guns demanded
extra pay, they had been adamant in their claim that contend-
ing with the four young Texans, particularly the Ysabel Kid,
required far greater caution than was previously considered
satisfactory. However, gazing about her, the *Comtesse* found
nothing to disturb her equanimity. None of the quartet were
showing even the slightest sign of suspecting something was
amiss.

One of the elements of the plot had been a nightly ritual
established during the journey from Corpus Christie. Every
evening, at Charlene and Ludwig von Farlenheim's instiga-
tion, dinner was served with Amelia Benkinsop and herself
seated at each end of the collapsible table. Acceding to the
suggestion, the Crown Prince had decreed that he, Dusty Fog,
Mark Counter, Colonel Liebenfrau, Major the Baron von
Goeringwald, their host and his nephew—after the captain
had carried out his duty as First Taster—alternated their seat-
ing positions to give them all the privilege of being next to the
ladies. There had been no objections from the conspirators, as
they had seen the arrangement would benefit them when the
time came to spring the trap. Although the Kid and Waco had
been invited to join the party, they had stated that they would
prefer to eat with Florence Drakefield and the Bosgravnian
orderlies.

The owner of the medicine show on the pretence of wanting to move on to carry out another engagement had asked if
he could give his performance before his audience began their
dinner. In addition to giving his consent, the Crown Prince
had shown his usual consideration—as the conspirators had
anticipated he would—by stating that the meal would be delayed to let all the party see the show. So Waco, the Kid, the
maid and the orderlies were standing at the rear of the table

where it was essential they, especially the two Texans, should be.

Broad in proportion to his slightly less than medium height, Doctor Seraphin was an impressive figure. Yet, in spite of his top hat, flowing black cloak lined with red silk and raiment suitable for a formal social gathering, his neatly bearded face had the tanned texture of one who spent much of his life in the open. Despite a certain hardness about his features, and the fact that he carried a pearl-handled Colt Cavalry Peacemaker in a cross-draw holster on the left side of the gunbelt which was not in accord with the rest of his attire, there was nothing to suggest he might be other than a very competent medicine showman. Having carried out a bombastic—yet entertaining—peroration extolling the virtues of "Doctor Seraphin's Elixir of Health and the High John Conquer root," he had announced that he would demonstrate the qualities of manual dexterity that taking them regularly had bestowed upon him. Then he began to march in a flamboyantly impressive manner towards his garishly painted wagon. With one exception, his performance had held the attention of his audience as it was meant to do.

As Waco had demonstrated in the past—and would continue to do—he was possessed of an inborn faculty for observation and deduction. When he noticed an item was out of the ordinary, even though the exact reason might elude him at the time, he never entirely forgot it. That had been the case when he had seen the *Comtesse* and her companion returning from the hunt. His every instinct had suggested that something was wrong, but he had been unable to decide exactly what it might be. Certainly it was not the fact that she had selected Alex von Farlenheim to accompany her when she left the camp. Since learning the truth about Dusty's separation from the rest of the floating outfit at Brownsville, she had displayed a growing coolness towards them. So he had drawn no other conclusion than to wonder whether her preference for the Bosgravnian was intended to make Mark jealous, or to repay the blond giant for not having told her the truth about the small Texan. Or it could be that, if she had forsaken her associates, she wanted an influential friend when she returned to Europe.

Nor, remembering the First Taster's adherence to the duties

of his office, had the youngster found anything suspicious in seeing him enter the wagon which carried the stores instead of joining the rest of the party at the table. Charlene and he had not returned until the others were about to sit down and, even though the dinner was to be delayed until the performance was over, the table had been set and he was anticipating that the Crown Prince might want to take a drink while it was taking place.

For all that, Waco had been unable to shake off the feeling that he was missing something of vital importance. It was not a sensation he found conducive to relaxation or peace of mind. In fact, it continued to nag at him with such persistence that it distracted him continually when he should have been engrossed in the masterly display of a medicine showman's art.

Watching von Farlenheim throw aside the stopper of the bottle he was carrying and start to walk towards the table, Waco was presented with another puzzle. While the night was dark, there was sufficient light thrown by several strategically placed lanterns and the lamps on the table to illuminate the majority of the camp site. So he noticed that the discarded object glistened in a fashion alien to a piece of cork as it fell and bounced on the ground. He was reminded of a how a small crystal ball had sparkled while it was being twirled before him as a man had attempted to hypnotize him.[1] Yet he had never seen a bottle of liquor intended for human consumption secured with anything other than a cork. Certainly none of those which had previously been brought from the wagon had had glass stoppers. To the best of his knowledge, only one kind of substance required such a means of retaining it.

A confirmation that he was thinking along the right lines came from seeing that von Farlenheim was not adhering to his usual routine. When carrying out the duty on the previous occasions, he had always delivered the bottle wrapped in a white cloth. That he was not now drew Waco's attention to the careful way in which he was handling the bottle. His right hand was around the neck and the left grasped the bottom, ensuring it was kept erect and none of its contents would spill.

Just as the youngster reached that point in his observations,

1. Told in: SET A-FOOT.—*J.T.E.*

something else caught his eye and he felt as if he had been doused by a jet of ice-cold water. At last he realized what had first aroused his sense of perturbation.

The weapon in von Farlenheim's holster was a *Colt Cavalry Model Peacemaker*!

It should have been the British-made Adams .450 sidearm that the Bosgravnian had insisted was superior to any single-action revolver!

Waco's speculations began to formulate into accurate deductions, beginning with the remembrance that Fritz von Farlenheim's younger cousin had been almost his exact double and had owned a Colt Cavalry Peacemaker.

Yet Alex von Farlenheim was supposed to have been drowned on the way to Brownsville!

If the report had been false, it could only have been made with Ludwig von Farlenheim's co-operation. He had admitted that the captain of the ship had been associated with him in running cargoes through the Union's blockade during the War Between the States and there was no doubt that he had received the telegraph message.

There could be only one reason for the pretence that Alex had been killed. So that he could be sustituted for his cousin. Fritz's duties as First Taster placed him in an ideal position to poison the Crown Prince. However, unless the noxious potion was slow in its action, to carry out such a deed would result in Alex's apprehension as soon as the effects were noticed. If Waco's theory regarding the contents of the bottle were correct, there would be no doubt of it as soon as Rudolph took a drink. He could not believe that the young Bosgravnian would be willing to sacrifice himself in such a manner.

An alternative sprang to the youngster's fertile mind!

Its concept was alarming!

Unless there was a diversion, Alex would be arrested immediately he had carried out his assignment.

So there would be a diversion!

It could only come from one place!

Ludwig von Farlenheim had done more than organize his younger nephew's supposed death and substitution for Fritz, he had arranged for Doctor Seraphin to come and entertain the hunting party. As was usually the case with members of his profession, the medicine showman had arrived in his distinctively painted wagon.

The site of the camp had been selected so that, particularly with the Ysabel Kid present, it would be practically impossible for intruders to approach even at night without being detected. Yet, in spite of being large enough to carry several passengers inside it, the wagon had not been searched when it arrived.

With the conclusions drawn, Waco had to decide what action he should take.

And quickly!

Von Farlenheim was approaching the table and Seraphin had almost reached the wagon.

Although Waco had helped to unhitch the team and tether them with the hunting party's animals, he had not paid any great attention to the vehicle. Now he noticed something that had sinister implications in the light of his deductions. He had anticipated a slight delay while the men he felt sure were concealed in it leapt out at the ends, but realized that this might not be necessary.

The wagon had the general appearance of a fair-sized delivery van, in that it had a rectangular wooden box-shaped body instead of a canvas canopy. Embellished with the owner's name and advertising his wares, the side panel could be lowered to form a counter. Unless the youngster missed his guess, the cord attached to the bolt at the top ran along to pass around a pulley, then hung down at the rear, which allowed it to be opened quickly.

"Here goes," Waco mused. "If I'm wrong, I'll get hell!" While delivering the observation to himself, he swung to face von Farlenheim. Flashing down, his right hand brought the Army Colt from its holster, cocked the hammer and pointed the barrel at the treacherous Bosgravnian, yelling, "Drop that bottle. Men in the wagon, Dusty!"

A moment later, the erstwhile peaceful scene erupted into sudden, violent motion!

First every head turned in the youngster's direction!

Then each person began to react!

All Waco's doubts were swept away as he saw how the young Bosgravnian responded. It established in no uncertain manner that he was correct in the assumption that Alex had been substituted for Fritz. While the latter might have shown alarm, his expression would not also have registered such a look of guilt inspired fury.

"He knows!" Alex screeched, raising the bottle with the intention of hurling it at the youngster.

Hearing what was being said, Seraphin had paused and looked around. Seeing what was happening, he sprang onwards with his right hand reaching for the cord that allowed the wagon's side panel to fall open.

The original plan had called for the showman to wait until Alex had presented the Crown Prince with hydrochloric acid instead of the expected white wine. Then Seraphin was to produce a drink he had concealed on his person and propose a toast to the royal visitor and the United States of America. Not until the effects of the deadly corrosive liquid was distracting everybody else's attention would he have pulled the cord and allow the four men in the vehicle to make use of their ten gauge shotguns.

The scheme had been arranged in such a fashion primarily to deal with the four members of Ole Devil's floating outfit. Their well deserved reputation for capability in matters *pistolero* made it imperative that they were disposed of quickly and before they could go into action themselves. Once the shooting started, half a dozen more hired guns would dash from their hiding places and help with the slaughter. Finally the camp would be looted and the blame would be put by the *Comtesse* and the von Farlenheims—who would claim they escaped because they had not returned from hunting when the attack was launched—upon a mythical gang of Mexican *bandidos*.

At least, that was what should have happened!

Unfortunately for the conspirators, the keen eyes, memory and deductive ability of the floating outfit's youngest member had prevented the surprise attack from succeeding.

Knowing Waco, Dusty and Mark realized he was not indulging in a practical joke. So, having looked at him, they swung their gaze in the direction he had suggested. While doing so, each of them was pleased that he was seated at the side of the table closest to the medicine show's wagon. They had turned their chairs towards it and there was nothing to prevent them from rising hurriedly, with hands leaping to the butts of their Colts.

All the other people at the table were rising with alacrity and reaching for weapons!

As her hand closed around the butt of the Webley R.I.C., Charlene darted a look of alarm at Ludwig von Farlenheim. He too was displaying angry consternation at the suggestion that their scheme was going wrong, but that did not prevent him reaching swiftly towards the Smith & Wesson Russian revolver he was wearing.

Displaying the kind of coolness that had been in evidence in other moments of danger, Amelia sent her chair toppling over as she sprang to her feet and started to pull out her Webley R.I.C. She was directing her attention to the woman at the other end of the table.

Caught just as unawares as everybody else by Waco's behaviour, the Kid moved as swiftly as his two *amigos*. Although he was standing within a few feet of the youngster and saw what von Farlenheim was doing, he did not offer to intervene. Satisfied that Waco could take care of himself, the Kid rotated his right hand to enfold the walnut grip and twist the heavy old Dragoon Colt from leather as he lunged forward.

Suspecting that the bottle held some form of acid, which had necessitated the use of a glass stopper instead of a cork, the youngster did not hesitate when he saw he was being threatened by it. His forefinger had already depressed the Colt's trigger and all he needed to do was remove his thumb from the hammer. Swinging forward, it set the firing cycle into motion.

Before Alex could carry out his intention, Waco's Colt thundered. By accident rather than deliberate aim, the bullet struck and shattered through the bottle on its way into the Bosgravnian's chest. In addition to the pain inflicted by the lead, much of the acid, so suddenly released, sprayed over him. Screaming in agony as it began to burn, he toppled backwards.

With his left hand grasping and tugging at the cord and the right beginning to pull free his Colt, Seraphin glanced over his shoulder. What he discovered warned him that not only was the plan misfiring badly, but his own life was now in jeopardy. So, as the well-greased bolt slid open and liberated the panel, he leapt towards the darkness beyond the wagon.

Although the hired killers in the vehicle were holding their shotguns, they had not been able to see what was happening outside. Their instructions were to be ready to go into action when they heard Seraphin proposing a toast to the Crown Prince and the commotion that would follow the words. While the disturbance had arisen, their leader had not delivered his signal. So, despite the sound of Waco's shot, they were taken unprepared when the panel began to tilt downwards. Nor did the sight which met their gaze improve the state of affairs. Colts in hand, two men who were acknowledged as high among the most deadly gun-fighters in Texas were running towards them.

Discovering without surprise that the danger Waco had implied in his cryptic utterance was materializing, Dusty and Mark were aware that there was only one way in which they might cope with it. Continuing their advance, each of them began to fire the weapons he had drawn with speed and commendable accuracy. Muzzle blasts appeared to be continuous red glows as their Colts turned loose a holocaust of lead upon the men in the wagon. Already alarmed by the turn of events which none of them had envisaged, not one of the discomforted quartet was able to line his shotgun much less discharge it at the proposed targets. Each of them took lead as he was trying to make corrections to the drastically changed conditions. Struck by the second bullet from Mark's left hand Colt, the man at the right screeched and spun around to discharge his shotgun's load into his nearest companion thus adding to the party's troubles. Apart from that, all four were felled without being permitted to put their weapons to use.

As was always the case in a precarious situation, the Kid forgot his white upbringing and reverted to the training he had been given to make him worthy of membership in the *Pehnane* Comanche Dog Soldier war lodge. It had converted him into a warrior second to none. Hurling himself between Liebenfrau and von Goeringwald, neither of whom was anywhere near as ready to take action, he bounded on to the table. By the time he landed, his left hand had joined the right to elevate the Dragoon Colt to shoulder level and he had assessed where it would be most advantageously put to use.

Barely conscious that, having exchanged glances with him, the *Comtesse* had decided discretion was the better part of valour and was turning to run away, Ludwig von Farlenheim was bringing up his Smith & Wesson with the intention of carrying out his mission to kill Crown Prince Rudolph no matter what the cost to himself. He was hardly aware of the menacing black-clad figure that seemed to materialize out of thin air on the table and swivel from the waist towards him. There was a brilliant red glow and a thunderous bellow as, powered by no less than fifty grains of prime du Pont black powder, the old Dragoon flung a .44 calibre ball of soft lead in his direction. It came into contact with the centre of his forehead, shattering through his brain and burst from the back of his head to kill him instantly.

Cocking the four pound, one ounce, thumb-busting giant of a handgun on its recoil, the Kid knew it would not be required to take further measures against von Farlenheim. His gaze swung away and, noticing what Seraphin was doing now that he had released the panel of the wagon, he launched himself from the table to give chase.

Extracting her Webley R.I.C. and drawing its hammer to fully cocked, Amelia did not allow herself to be distracted by what was going on around her. Looking past the Kid as he was leaping onto the table, she saw that Charlene was starting to run away. With the thundering of the three Texans' Colts echoing in her ears, she set off in pursuit. Darting between Rudolph, Liebenfrau, the Baron and the rest of the royal retinue while they were still drawing their weapons, she ran swiftly after the departing woman.

"Charlene!"

Hearing her name as she was leaving the lighted area of the camp site, the *Comtesse* looked behind her. Cold rage swept through her as she discovered that the Englishwoman who had inflicted a painful and humiliating defeat over her was following her. Such was the fury inspired by the sight that she forgot her intention of joining the rest of Seraphin's hired killers and, if she could not persuade them to launch an attack upon the hunting party, joining them in their flight.

"God damn you!" Charlene shrieked in her native tongue, as she halted, turned, and brought up her revolver with the speed of determined desperation.

Even if Amelia had not been able to understand French, she would have known that her life was threatened. She had seen Charlene shoot and knew that she was at a distance where the *Comtesse* could be counted upon not to miss. Coming to a stop, she adopted a similar technique to that of the Kid by raising the Webley with both hands.

Charlene was employing the same aid to accuracy, but there was one major and vital difference in what came next. The Webley R.I.C. had a double action mechanism which did not need to be cocked manually, but could be fired by squeezing the trigger. However, Amelia had drawn back the hammer and the *Comtesse* had not. So, although their shooting skill was practically equal, she had a slight—yet vital—advantage in that she required less exertion to discharge her weapon.

Both revolvers went off at almost the same instant!

Even as Amelia saw Charlene jerk under the impact of her bullet, she felt herself struck on the left side. Crying out involuntarily as the searing pain bit into her, she dropped her revolver and, as the *Comtesse* twirled around and then fell to the ground, she clutched at the source of the agony. Her questing hands became wet by the blood that was flowing from the furrow carved across her flesh.

"Whooee!" Dusty breathed, as the last of the four men in the wagon disappeared from view, looking at Mark. "*That* was close!"

"I don't want anything closer," the blond giant replied. "If the boy hadn't yelled when he did—!"

"Yes," the small Texan agreed, having no need for his *amigo* to finish the comment. Glancing to where the Kid was running by, he looked around to find out what the rest of the party was doing. "He saved our lives, for sure. The young cuss won't be fit to live with for weeks after this."

CHAPTER SIXTEEN

You Hired Beguinage

"All right, Captain Fog," Colonel Wilhelm Liebenfrau said, as he and the small Texan came to a halt about fifteen feet from the edge of the small clearing they had entered. "Why did you ask me to come for a stroll with you?"

"I figured that it was time you and I had a talk," Dusty replied. "And, considering what it's about, I reckoned *you'd* prefer we did it somewhere private."

It was shortly after noon on the day after Charlene, *Comtesse de* Petain and her confederates had carried out their abortive attempt to assassinate Crown Prince Rudolph of Bosgravnia.

Of the would-be assassins, only Alex von Farlenheim and one of the men in the wagon had been alive when the guns stopped roaring. The cost to their prospective victims was the bullet wound, which had resulted in a broken rib, sustained by Amelia Benkinsop. To give Doctor Seraphin his due, he had warned the rest of his companions that the scheme had failed. He had been yelling for them to bring him a horse so he could flee with them when he heard the Ysabel Kid coming. Turning, he had made the fatal mistake of missing with his shot at the black-dressed Texan and was not granted an opportunity to remedy the error. A bullet from the old Dragoon Colt had written *finis* to his career as medicine showman and unsuspected professional killer.

When sending the Kid and Waco to inform the sheriff of Duval County about the incident, Dusty had also instructed them to bring back medical assistance for the injured. Not only had they returned from San Diego with the peace officer and a doctor, they had been accompanied by a woman. She had claimed to be a trained nurse who was passing through the town, having arrived that morning, on her way to take up an appointment in a San Antonio hospital.

Although Alex's wound had been fatal, he had refused to supply Liebenfrau with the names of the other members of the Council of Noble Birth in Bosgravnia. He had died before the doctor arrived, cursing the Crown Prince, the Personal Attendant and declaring they would never find his cousin alive. Apart from telling his captors where the First Taster could be found, the hired killer had not been able to do more than explain how the assassination was to be carried out. Following the instructions they had been given, Mark Counter, Major the Baron von Goeringwald and Captain von Farlenheim's orderly had located him. Stripped to his underwear, bound, gagged and suffering from a concussion, he had been brought back to the camp. According to the doctor on examining him, he would not suffer any serious after effects as a result of his experience.

Once the various formalities had been completed, Dusty had asked Liebenfrau to accompany him for a walk. They had made their way to where bushes lined the banks of the stream which supplied the camp with water. It was about half a mile from the site and, as the hired killers had pointed out when learning what was expected of them, the nearest cover to it. Neither the small Texan nor the Personal Attendant had spoken until they arrived in the clearing and the latter raised the point which he had been considering since he had received the request from the small Texan. Nor had either of them been as alert as they should have been as each was engrossed in his thoughts.

"That sounds almost ominous," Liebenfrau remarked, but there was no levity in his manner and he speculatively eyed the young man for whom he had developed a great respect.

"It could well be all of that," Dusty admitted. "Depends on whether I'm right about the reason why *you* hired Beguinage."

"I?" the Personal Attendant repeated, his hard face showing no emotion. "Why would I hire him?"

"I *could* be wrong," the small Texan replied, standing apparently relaxed yet as ready for instant action as a compressed coil spring. "But I don't reckon it was to have him kill His Highness."

"Thank you for *that*," Liebenfrau said gruffly, but with obvious sincerity. "But how did you know I had hired him?"

"Neither the *Comtesse's* crowd nor the anarchists had, so it had to be somebody else," Dusty explained. "I couldn't decide who until his woman started trying to kill off those she blamed for his death and you were one of us she had a try at. Then I noticed how you got sort of edgy when you were asked what you knew about Beguinage and that made me reckon I was on the right track. Waco allowed that he was figuring on the same lines when I talked to him about it."

"You are both very shrewd young men," Liebenfrau complimented. "And I suppose that you know why I hired him?"

"I've a fair notion," Dusty drawled, the Bosgravnian's second sentence having been more of a statement than a question. "He was Europe's 'premier assassin' by his and all your accounts. So you wanted to make sure nobody else hired him to kill the Prince. His chore was to take out anybody who looked likely to be after His Highness, but he was to make folks think he'd been paid to do it himself."

"The last part was *his* idea," Liebenfrau corrected. "From what I was given to understand, he thought it might have an adverse effect upon his future career if it became known that he had been hired to stop other people killing somebody."

"And you went along with it as you didn't take to the notion of folks hearing you knew how to get hold of 'n' hire a longhorn like Beguinage," Dusty guessed dryly.

"A man in my position must know many things," the Personal Attendant pointed out, without any suggestion of annoyance. "And use even unfair means to do my duty."

"Why sure," Dusty conceded. "Not that I regret having done it, mind, but I wouldn't have had to kill him if I'd known what he'd been hired to do."

"You will have cause to regret having done it," a hard feminine voice with a trace of an undefinable foreign accent stated.

Taking a step to the right as Liebenfrau turned, Dusty looked at the speaker. Although his left hand had started to reach for the off side Colt, he stopped the movement with his fingers a few inches from the bone handle. As he had known from the voice, the woman who was standing partially concealed behind a bush had accompanied the doctor from San Diego in the capacity of nurse. About five foot seven in height, somewhat bulkily built and clad in a plain black two-piece travelling costume, he decided that there was something vaguely familiar about her. It was not her bland, matronly features. Nothing about them was eye-catching or memorable. However, the Winchester Model of 1873 carbine she was holding with the butt cradled against her right shoulder was handled with every evidence of competence.

"You were very wise to stop, Captain Fog," the woman stated, lining the carbine with disconcerting steadiness at the centre of the small Texan's chest. "Or should I say 'Mr. *Rapido* Clint'?"

"I thought he'd be gone and forgotten now I've got my hair back to its natural colour," Dusty replied, studying the "nurse" with greater attention than he had paid to her until that moment.

"I'll *never* forget *you*, or forgive you for what you've done," the woman declared, gritting out the words. Then her voice took on a more mocking tone and she continued, "As I said, you were wise not to try to draw the pistol. I'm going to kill you anyway, but I want you to know who I am first."

"Give me a chance and I'll make a right smart guess at *that*," Dusty answered. "And when it comes to killing me, you'll need to be a better shot with that saddlegun than you were with that thing you used to throw the knife at the Colonel."

"*She* threw it at me?" Liebenfrau barked, swinging his gaze to the small Texan. Not only did he display surprise, but puzzlement tinged his voice as he went on, "But I thought that was done by Beguinage's woman!"

"It was," Dusty confirmed, without taking his eyes from the "nurse." "At least by one of them. Only mistake I made was not figuring he might have two working for him."

"You have made other mistakes, too," the woman corrected, with a hint of asperity.

"Only little-bitty ones," Dusty countered, adopting a manner redolent of smug condescension as he had noticed that the annoyance came when he spoke of the women working for Beguinage. "I didn't recognize either you or the other girl as the nuns who were outside my room at the Portside Hotel the day I shot the snake *he* left there. But then, whoever notices what a nun looks like."

"Who indeed?" the woman agreed, but her tone suggested she was finding the small Texan's attitude irritating. "Certainly nobody suspected *me* of leaving the snake, either in your room or to kill that man in Brownsville."

"*He* must have taught you what to do," Dusty drawled, waiting for the first chance he was offered to turn the tables and sensing he was taking the right line to bring it about. "Which I'm lucky I put him down, though. What I've seen and heard of *him*, he wouldn't've let you-all make the fool mistakes you've pulled since he was dead."

"You think not?" the woman hissed. "Then that is another mistake your so-great intelligence has made! Alphonse was my son and *I* am the Beguinage!"

"*You*?" Dusty scoffed and there was the world of disbelief in the way he said the single word.

Although the woman's forefinger began to tighten on the carbine's trigger, she refrained from completing its pressure. Almost writhing in the fury that had been aroused by the way she was being underrated by such a small and insignificant looking person, she wanted him to learn he was not as brilliant as he clearly imagined himself to be. Her pride was wounded deeply by his comments, for she knew them to be completely wrong as far as her position in their organization was concerned.

On being ordered to leave her convent, having been caught in an act of misconduct with a visiting priest that had resulted in the birth of twins, the woman[1] had turned to the life of a professional assassin. In addition to becoming an expert in her

1. Neither "Cap" Fog nor Miss Amelia P. D. Benkinsop, M.A., B.SC. (Oxon), George Medal, Honorary Member, Holloway Old Girls' Association—see Chapter Eleven, Footnote One—with whom the author also consulted, could find any record of "Beguinage's" real name. Incidentally, according to the researches of fictionist-genealogist Philip José Farmer—author of the biographical works TARZAN ALIVE and DOC SAVAGE, *His Apocalyptic Life*—no matter who her father might be, the eldest girl of each succeeding generation retained the name Amelia Penelope Diana Benkinsop.—*J.T.E.*

new trade and building the organization which had kept her identity a secret, she had trained her children to be extremely capable assistants. It had been with a sense of malicious humour that she had adopted the name given to members of the Catholic lay sisterhood from which she was expelled.[2]

Over the years, the Beguinage had rarely failed on an assignment. That they should have done so and in such a disastrous fashion while operating in a country which the woman had regarded as barbarous and poorly educated, when the police of every European nation had been unable to even identify them, made the defeat all the more bitter. So she had sworn to be avenged upon those whom she held to be most responsible. Having had no greater respect than Dusty for the ability of Marshal Benjamin Digbry, she had killed him to regain possession of her son's knife and, more important, because of a shortage of the poison which was contained in the pot. Wishing to terminate the affair as quickly as possible, she had told her daughter to hire a second party of men to kill the small Texan while she went to take care of Liebenfrau, who she had anticipated would visit the livery barn on arriving at Corpus Christie. Having seen the preparations being made by the Texans, she had deduced the precautions they were intending to take, even to the splitting up of the party for the journey to the town.

Deciding to withhold from further activities for a time after her daughter's death, so as to lull her victims into a sense of false security, the woman had followed half a day or so behind the hunting party. As they had stuck to the stagecoach trail until approaching San Diego, this had not been difficult. On her arrival at the town, the story she had spread about being a nurse so as to avoid attracting unwanted attention had paid an unexpected dividend. She was asked by the doctor to accompany him to the camp, supplying a perfect reason for her to go there. Seeing Dusty and Liebenfrau setting off for a walk and noticing the direction they were taking, she had collected her Winchester from the buckboard in which she was travelling

---

2. The Beguine order, which originated in the Netherlands during the Twelfth Century, is devoted to a religious life, but not bound by irrevocable vows.—*J.T.E.*

and had slipped away unnoticed to follow them. She was confident that they were sufficiently far from the rest of the party for her to be able to use the weapon without the shots being heard, and she hoped to be on her way to safety before they were missed.

"*Me!*" the woman insisted. "Alphonse and Arelette were *my* assistants. It was I who taught them all they knew about kill—!" The words died away as she noticed that the Personal Attendant's right hand had moved until it was in position to open the flap of his holster. Her voice hardened, but she kept the carbine pointing at Dusty while going on, "Don't do that, Colonel. I mean *you* no harm!"

"Oh come on now, ma'am," the small Texan protested. "You know you're lying in your teeth. You're not about to leave *anybody* alive who knows who and what you are."

"I agree with Captain Fog," Liebenfrau declared.

"There now," Dusty said triumphantly, but stood as motionless as he had from the moment his hand had halted its reach for the Colt. "That gives you-all one hell of a problem, lady. You can't shoot us both at the same time and, while you're throwing lead my way, the Colonel's going to get his gun and drop you where you stand."

"I swear to you—!" the woman began, turning her gaze to the Personal Attendant.

"Liar!" Liebenfrau thundered and took a step forward, flipping open the hoster's flap to grip the butt of his revolver.

Before she could prevent herself, the woman started to swing the carbine in the Bosgravnian's direction. Her instincts gave a warning that he was not the greatest danger, but it arrived just a fraction too late.

Using the lightning fast and deadly reactions which had so often saved his life in the past, Dusty brought out the left side Colt. Only once before had he been compelled to shoot a member of the opposite sex, but he felt no compunction over having to repeat what was just as essential an act of self-preservation.[3] Nor, distasteful as the thought might be, dare he do other than shoot for an instantaneous kill. Already the carbine was reversing the move that had been taking it away from

3. The incident is told in: THE BAD BUNCH.—*J.T.E.*

him. To hesitate would allow it to be aligned and she would not delay firing any longer.

Just over half a second after the small Texan had been presented with the chance to complete the reach for his Colt, it was out, sending a bullet that grazed by the carbine and entered the woman's left eye. Despite being thrown backwards, she squeezed the trigger and the lead discharged by her weapon hissed by within an inch of Dusty's head.

'*Gracias*, Colonel," Dusty said quietly, starting to walk forward.

"It was the least I could do to repay you," Liebenfrau replied, following the small Texan towards the bushes.

"Well, one thing's for sure," Dusty stated, as he and the Personal Attendant looked at the motionless figure sprawled on the ground. "This time, Beguinage *is* dead!"

Appendix One

During the War Between the States, at the age of seventeen, Dustine Edward Marsden "Dusty" Fog had won promotion in the field and was put in command of Company "C" Texas Light Cavalry.[1] Leading them during the Arkansas Campaign, he had earned the reputation for being an exceptionally capable military raider and a worthy contemporary for the South's other leading exponents, John Singleton Mosby and Turner Ashby.[2] In addition to preventing a pair of pro-Union fanatics from starting an Indian uprising which would have decimated most of Texas,[3] he had supported Belle Boyd, the Rebel Spy,[4] on two of her most dangerous assignments.[5]

When the War had finished, he had become the segundo of the great OD Connected ranch in Rio Hondo County, Texas. Its owner and his uncle, General Jackson Baines "Ole Devil" Hardin had been crippled in a riding accident,[6] placing much responsibility—including handling an important mission upon which the good relations between the United States and Mexico had hung in the balance[7]—upon his young shoulders. After helping to gather horses to replenish the ranch's depleted

---

1. Told in: YOU'RE IN COMMAND NOW, MR. FOG.
2. Told in: THE BIG GUN; UNDER THE STARS AND BARS; THE FASTEST GUN IN TEXAS and KILL DUSTY FOG!
3. Told in: THE DEVIL GUN.
4. Further details of Belle Boyd's career are given in: THE HOODED RIDERS; THE BAD BUNCH; TO ARMS, TO ARMS IN DIXIE!; THE SOUTH WILL RISE AGAIN; THE REMITTANCE KID and THE WHIP AND THE WAR LANCE.
5. Told in: THE COLT, THE SABRE and THE REBEL SPY.
6. Told in the "The Paint" episode of THE FASTEST GUN IN TEXAS.
7. Told in: THE YSABEL KID.

171

remuda,[8] he had been sent to assist Colonel Charles Goodnight on the trail drive to Fort Sumner, New Mexico, which
had done much to help the Lone Star State to recover from the
impoverished conditions left by the War.[9] With that achieved,
he had been equally successful in helping Goodnight convince
other ranchers it would be possible to drive large herds of
cattle to the railroad in Kansas.[10]

Having proven himself to be a first-class cowhand, Dusty
went on to become acknowledged as a very capable trail boss,[11]
round-up captain,[12] and town taming lawman.[13] Competing in a
revolver handling competition at the Cochise County Fair, he
won the title, "The Fastest Gun In The West," by beating many
other experts in the *pistolero* line.[14] In later years, following his
marriage to Lady Winifred Amelia "Freddie Woods" Besgrove-
Woodstole,[15] he became a notable diplomat.

Dusty Fog never found his lack of stature an impediment.
In addition to being naturally strong, he had taught himself to
be completely ambidextrous. Possessing perfectly attuned reflexes, he could draw either or both of his Colts—whether of
the 1860 Army Model[16] or their improved successors, the

8. Told in: .44 CALIBRE MAN and A HORSE CALLED MOGOLLON.
9. Told in: GOODNIGHT'S DREAM (Bantam edition title THE FLOATING
OUTFIT) and FROM HIDE AND HORN.
10. Told in: SET TEXAS BACK ON HER FEET and THE HIDE AND TALLOW
MEN.
11. Told in: TRAIL BOSS.
12. Told in: THE MAN FROM TEXAS.
13. Told in: QUIET TOWN; THE MAKING OF A LAWMAN; THE TROUBLE
BUSTERS; THE SMALL TEXAN and THE TOWN TAMERS.
14. Told in: GUN WIZARD.
15. Their grandson, Alvin Dustine "Cap" Fog became the finest combat
pistol shot of his generation and the youngest man ever to become a
captain in the Texas Rangers, see: "CAP" FOG, TEXAS RANGER, MEET MR. J.
G. REEDER and "CAP" FOG, COMPANY "Z".
16. Although the military sometimes claimed derisively that it was easier
to kill a sailor than a soldier, the weight factor of the respective weapons
had caused the United States' Navy to adopt a revolver of .36 calibre
while the Army employed one of .44. The weapon would be carried on a
seaman's belt and not—handguns having originally and primarily been
developed for use by cavalry—on the person or saddle of a man who
would be doing most of his travelling on the back of a horse. Therefore,
.44 became known as the "Army" calibre and .36 as the "Navy."

"Peacemakers"[17]—with lightning speed and great accuracy.
Old Devil Hardin's valet, Tommy Okasi,[18] was Japanese and a
trained *Samurai*[19] and from him Dusty had learned *ju-jitsu* and
karate.[20] Neither had received the publicity they were given in
later years and were little known in the Western Hemisphere at
that time. So the knowledge was very useful when he had to
fight bare-handed against larger, heavier and stronger men.

17. Introduced in 1873 as the Colt Model P "Single Action Army" revolver, but more generally referred to as the "Peacemaker," production
was continued until 1941 when it was taken out of the line to make way
for more modern weapons required for World War II. Over *three hundred
and fifty thousand* were manufactured in practically every handgun calibre—with the exception of the .41 and .44 Magnums, which were not
developed during the production period—from .22 Short rimfire to .476
Eley. However, the majority fired either .45 or .44.40; the latter allowing
the same ammunition to be used in the Winchester Model of 1873 rifle.
    The barrel lengths were from three inches in the "Storekeeper" Model,
which did not have an extractor rod, to the sixteen inches of the so-called
"Buntline Special." The latter was offered with an attachable metal skele-
ton butt stock so it could be used as a carbine. The main barrel lengths
were: Cavalry, seven and a half inches; Artillery, five and a half inches;
Civilian, four and three-quarter inches.
    Popular demand, said to have been caused by the upsurge of action-
escapism-adventure Western series on television, brought the Peacemaker
back into production in 1955 and it is still in the line.
18. "Tommy Okasi" is an Americanized corruption of the name he gave
when picked up from a derelict vessel in the China Sea by a ship under the
command of General Hardin's father, but no record of the actual Japanese
name exists.
19. When asked by the author at Fort Worth, Texas, in 1975, why a
trained *Samurai* was compelled to flee from his homeland, Alvin Dustine "Cap" Fog said that, because of the circumstances and the high social
standing of the people involved—all of whom have descendants holding
positions of importance and influence in Japan at the time of writing—
that the Hardin, Fog and Blaze clan consider it is inadvisable even at this
late date to make the facts public. Details of how Tommy made use of his
Samurai training are given in the "Ole Devil Hardin" series, which also
covers much of the General's early life.
20. As is told in: KILL DUSTY FOG!; THE BAD BUNCH; MCGRAW'S INHERI-
TANCE; THE RIO HONDO WAR and GUNSMOKE THUNDER, General Hardin's
granddaughter, Betty, was also given instruction in *ju jitsu* and *karate* by
Tommy Okasi and gained considerable proficiency.

Appendix Two

With his exceptional good looks and magnificent physical development, Mark Counter presented the kind of appearance which many people expected of Dusty Fog. It was a fact of which they took advantage when the need arose[1] and at least once was almost the cause of Mark being killed in mistake for Dusty.[2]

While serving as a lieutenant under General Bushrod Sheldon's command in the War Between the States, Mark's merits as an efficient and courageous officer had been overshadowed by his taste in uniforms. Always a dandy, coming from a wealthy family had allowed him to indulge his whims. His clothing, particularly a skirtless tunic, had been much copied by the other young bloods of the Confederate States' Army despite considerable opposition and disapproval on the part of hide-bound senior officers.

When peace had come, Mark followed Sheldon to fight for Emperor Maximilian in Mexico. There he had met Dusty Fog and the Ysabel Kid, helping with the former's mission.[3] On returning to Texas, he had been invited to join the OD Connected's floating outfit.[4] Knowing his elder brothers could help his father, Big Rance, to run the R Over C ranch in the

1. One occasion is described in: THE SOUTH WILL RISE AGAIN.
2. One incident is told in: BEGUINAGE.
3. Told in: THE YSABEL KID.
4. "Floating outfit:" a group of four to six cowhands employed by a large ranch to work the more distant sections of the property. Taking food in a chuck wagon, or "greasy sack" on the back of a mule, they would be away from the ranch house for long periods. Because of General Jackson Baines "Ole Devil" Hardin's prominence in the affairs of Texas, the OD Connected's floating outfit were frequently sent to assist his friends who found themselves in trouble or endangered.

Big Bend country—and suspecting life would be more exciting with Dusty and the Kid—he had accepted.

An expert cowhand, Mark was known as Dusty's right bower.[5] He also gained acclaim by virtue of his enormous strength and ability in a rough-house brawl. However, due to being so much in the small Texan's company, his full potential as a gun-fighter received little attention. Men who were competent to judge such matters stated that he was second only to the Rio Hondo gun wizard in speed and accuracy.

Many women found Mark's appearance irresistible, including Miss Martha Jane Canary;[6] who was better known as "Calamity Jane."[7] In his younger days, only one—the lady outlaw, Belle Starr—held his heart.[8] It was not until several years after her death that he courted and married Dawn Sutherland[9] who he had first met on the Goodnight trail drive to Fort Sumner, New Mexico.[10]

5. "Right bower": second highest trump card in the game of euchre.
6. Mark's main meetings with Miss Martha Jane Canary are told in: TROUBLED RANGE; THE WILDCATS and THE FORTUNE HUNTERS.
7. Books in which Martha Jane Canary takes a leading role are: COLD DECK, HOT LEAD; CALAMITY SPELLS TROUBLE; TROUBLE TRAIL; THE COW THIEVES; WHITE STALLION, RED MARE (co-starring the Ysabel Kid); THE BIG HUNT (in which Mark Counter makes a guest appearance); THE WHIP AND THE WAR LANCE (co-starring Belle Boyd).
8. How Mark's romance with Belle Starr commenced, progressed and ended is recorded in in "The Bounty On Belle Starr's Scalp" episode of TROUBLED RANGE; RANGELAND HERCULES; the "The Lady Known As Belle" episode of THE HARD RIDERS and GUNS IN THE NIGHT. She also appears in HELL IN THE PALO DURO and GO BACK TO HELL, assisting Dusty Fog, the Ysabel Kid and Waco and in THE BAD BUNCH and THE QUEST FOR BOWIE'S BLADE.
9. Two of Mark's great-grandchildren, Deputy Sheriff Bradford Counter and James Allenvale "Bunduki" Gunn, achieved considerable fame on their own behalf. Details of the former's career as a peace officer are given in the Rockabye County series covering various aspects of modern law enforcement in Texas and the latter's life story is recorded in the Bunduki series.
10. The first meeting is described in: GOODNIGHT'S DREAM and FROM HIDE AND HORN.

Appendix Three

Raven Head, the only daughter of Chief Long Walker, war leader of the *Pehnane*—Wasp, Quick Stinger, or Raider—Comanches' Dog Soldier lodge and his French Creole *pairaivo*,[1] married an Irish Kentuckian adventurer, Sam Ysabel, but died giving birth to their first child. Baptized with the name, Loncey Dalton Ysabel, the boy was raised in the fashion of the *Nemenuh*.[2] With his father away on the family's combined business of mustanging—catching and breaking wild horses—and smuggling, his education had been left largely in the hands of his maternal grandfather.[3] From Long Walker, he had learned all those things a Comanche warrior must know: how to ride the wildest, freshly caught mustang, or when raiding—a polite name for the favourite *Nemenuh* sport of horse stealing—to subjugate domesticated mounts to his will; to follow the faintest tracks and conceal traces of his own passing;[4] to locate hidden enemies and keep out of sight himself when the need arose; to move in silence through the thickest cover, or on the darkest of nights and to be highly proficient in the use of a variety of weapons.

In all the subjects, the boy had proved an excellent pupil. He had inherited his father's Kentuckian rifle shooting skill and, while not real fast on the draw—taking slightly over a second, where a top hand could practically halve that time—

1. *Pairaivo:* first or favourite wife. As the case of the other Comanche names, this is a phonetic spelling.
2. *Nemenuh:* "The People," the Comanches' name for their nation. Members of the other Indian races with whom they came into contact called them the "*Tshaoh*," the "Enemy People."
3. Told in: COMANCHE.
4. An example of the Ysabel Kid's ability to conceal his tracks is given in the "The Half Breed" episode of THE HALF BREED.

he performed passably with his Colt Second Model Dragoon revolver. He had won his *Pehnane* man-name, *Cuchilo*—Spanish for "Knife"—by his exceptional skill in wielding one as a weapon. It was claimed that he could equal the alleged designer[5] in performing with the massive and special type of blade[6] which bore Colonel James Bowie's name.[7]

Joining his father on smuggling expeditions along the Rio Grande, the boy had become known to the Mexicans in the border country as *Cabrito*: a name which, although meaning a young goat, had come from hearing white men refer to him as the Ysabel Kid and was spoken *very* respectfully in such a context. Smuggling did not attract mild-mannered pacifists, but even the roughest and toughest of the bloody border's brood had acknowledged that it did not pay to rile up Sam Ysabel's son. The Kid's education and upbringing had not been calculated to develop an over-inflated sense of the sanctity of human life. When crossed, he dealt with the situation like a *Pehnane* Dog Soldier—to which war lodge of savage and efficient warriors he had been initiated and belonged—swiftly and in an effectively deadly manner.

During the War Between the States, the Kid and his father had commenced by riding as scouts for Dixie's "Grey Ghost,"

5. Some researchers claim that the actual designer of the knife was James Bowie's eldest brother, Rezin Pleasant. It was made by the master cutler, James Black, of Arkansas. (A few authorities state it was manufactured by Jesse Cliffe, a white blacksmith employed on the Bowie family's plantation in Rapides Parish Louisiana).

6. As all James Black's, q.v., bowie knives were hand-made, there were variations in their dimensions. The specimen owned by the Ysabel Kid had a blade eleven and a half inches long, two and a half inches wide and a quarter of an inch thick at the guard. According to W. D. "Bo" Randall of Randall Made Knives, Orlando, Florida—a master cutler and authority on the subject—Bowie's knife weighed forty three ounces, having a blade eleven inches long, two and a quarter inches wide and three-eighths of an inch thick. One thing they all had in common was a "clip" point, where the last few inches on the back of the blade joins the main cutting surface in a concave arc to become an extension of it.

7. What happened to James Bowie's knife after his death during the final assault at the siege of the Alamo Mission, San Antonio de Bexar, Texas, on 6th March, 1936, is told in: GET UREA and THE QUEST FOR BOWIE'S BLADE.

Colonel John Singleton Mosby. Later, their specialized knowledge and talents were converted to having them collect and deliver to the Confederate States' authorities in Texas supplies which had been run through the blockade imposed by the United States' Navy into Matamoros, or purchased elsewhere in Mexico. It had been hard and dangerous work, but never more so than on the two occasions when they had become involved in missions with Belle Boyd, the Rebel Spy.[8]

Soon after the end of the War, Sam Ysabel had been murdered. While hunting for the killers, the Kid had met Dusty Fog and Mark Counter.[9] When the mission which they had been engaged upon came to its successful conclusion, learning that the Kid no longer wished to follow the family business of smuggling, Dusty had offered him employment on the OD Connected ranch. It had been in the capacity as a scout, rather than a cowhand, that he was required and his talents were of great use as a member of the floating outfit. The Kid's acceptance had been of great benefit all round. The ranch obtained the services of an extremely capable and efficient man. Dusty had acquired a loyal friend who was ready to stick by him through any kind of danger. For his part, the Kid had turned from a life of petty crime—with the ever present danger of having his activities develop into serious law breaking—and became a most useful member of society. Peace officers and law abiding citizens might have found cause to feel thankful for that. His *Nemenuh* education would have made him a terrible and murderous outlaw if he had been driven to a life of criminal intent.

Obtaining his first repeating rifle while in Mexico with Dusty and Mark—a Winchester Model of 1866, nicknamed the "old yellowboy" because of its brass frame, although at the time known as the "New, Improved Henry"—the Kid had soon become acknowledged as a master in its use. At the Cochise County Fair in Arizona, he had won the first prize—one of the legendary Winchester Model of 1873 "One Of A Thousand" rifles—against stiff competition.[10]

8. Told in: THE BLOODY BORDER and BACK TO THE BLOODY BORDER.
9. Told in: THE YSABEL KID.
10. Told in: GUN WIZARD.

In part, it was through the Kid's efforts that the majority of the Comanche bands had agreed to go on to the reservation following the circumvented attempts to ruin the peace treaty meeting at Fort Sorrel.[11] Nor could Dusty have cleaned out the outlaw town of Hell without his assistance.[12]

11. Told in: SIDEWINDER.
12. Told in: HELL IN THE PALO DURO and GO BACK TO HELL.

Appendix Four

Left an orphan almost from birth by a Waco Indian raid, from whence had come the only name he knew, Waco had been raised as a member of a North Texas rancher's large family.[1] Guns had always been a part of his life and his sixteenth birthday had seen him riding with Clay Allison's tough, "wild onion" ranch crew. The CA hands, like their employer, were notorious for their wild ways and frequently dangerous behaviour. Living in the company of such men, all older than himself, he had grown quick to take offence and well able, even eager, to demonstrate his ability to draw at lightning speed and shoot very accurately. It had seemed to be only a matter of time before one shoot-out too many would have seen him branded as a killer and fleeing from the law with a price on his head.

Fortunately for Waco, that day did not come. From the moment Dusty Fog saved the youngster's life, at considerable risk to his own, a change for the better had come.[2] Leaving Allison, with the Washita curly wolf's blessing, Waco had become a member of the OD Connected's floating outfit. The other members of this élite group had treated him like a favourite younger brother and taught him many useful lessons. From the Ysabel Kid, he had learned to read tracks and generally act as a scout. Mark Counter gave him instruction in bare-handed combat. From a gambler of their acquaintance had come information about the ways of honest and crooked members of his profession. From Dusty Fog, he had gained the knowledge which—helped by an inborn flair for deduc-

1. How Waco repaid his obligation to Sunshine Sam Catlin, his adoptive father, is told in: WACO'S DEBT.
2. Told in: TRIGGER FAST.

tive reasoning—would help him to gain fame as a peace officer of exceptional merit.[3]

Benefiting from his education at his friends' hands, in later years Waco was to become an extremely competent and highly respected peace officer.[4] He served with distinction in the Arizona Rangers,[5] as sheriff of Two Forks County, Utah,[6] and finally held office as a U.S. Marshal.[7]

3. Told in: THE MAKING OF A LAWMAN and THE TROUBLE BUSTERS.
4. Early examples of Waco's ability as a peace officer are given in the "The Hired Butcher" episode of THE HARD RIDERS; the "A Tolerable Straight Shooting Gun" episode of THE FLOATING OUTFIT. (Corgi Books' edition title); THE SMALL TEXAN and THE TOWN TAMERS.
5. Told in: SAGEBRUSH SLEUTH; ARIZONA RANGER and WACO RIDES IN.
6. Told in: THE DRIFTER and, by inference, DOC LEROY, MD.
7. Told in: HOUND DOG MAN.